C.L. SMITH

Jensen Smith and the Immortals

First edition

Illustration by Alicia N. Mauk

This book was professionally typeset on Reedsy.
Find out more at reedsy.com

Contents

Prologue

Hello everyone, my name's Jensen. Jensen Smith; your everyday, normal beta. Now you might be wondering what a beta is. Well, in simple terms, a beta is a version of a werewolf. Yes, like fangs, claws, fur type werewolf. We're real, and we're around.

Now before you start going off on a tangent about how werewolves kill people and lose their minds on a full moon, you're only partially right. True, the original werewolves, I'm talking about the Immortals, way back when, some of them are still alive today; they would change into a full, giant wolf, at every full moon, terrorizing and killing everything and everyone in their path. Now, people who are bitten by one of the Immortals, not born like me, also lose control.

These days, most werewolves look like normal people. Like me for example; I look no different than any other fifteen-year-old kid. Heck, I even go to school, with normal people. Now, with that being said, our younglings do lose control on a full moon, however, most of them, given proper training, can control this change. I was able to control the change at the ripe old age of two. According to my mother, this was extremely young to master the change or shift, we call it.

There is another thing you have to understand as well, once we master the shift, we can summon our powers and abilities at will, without the aid of a full moon. Some of our powers, like our quick healing and strength, are always present, even before we master shifting. However, other powers, like our abilities to see in the dark, extend our claws and fangs, things like that, all come with training. The best of us though, after enough training and control, can shift at will, day or night, any time of the year.

With all of the explanations being out of the way now, we can finally get

iv

into the story. Because despite what you might be thinking, this isn't a story about how I'm a werewolf. This is a story about how I found out who my father was, and everything that happened after. So strap in.

1

Chapter One: The story begins

It started like any other day. I woke up in the morning before school, showered, got dressed, had breakfast, and got on the bus.

The school was more or less the same; friends, class, lunch, boredom, the usual. After school, however, is when things started to get weird.

My brother and sister decided to ride the bus home today. Which was strange, because they normally either ran home (we live about fifteen miles away) or rode with their friends. They got on the bus with strangely gleeful greetings.

"Hey, Jensen!" My brother Zak yelled with a smile when he saw me sitting in the back.

"Jensen! Happy birthday!" Stephanie, my sister, yelled as well, sitting next to my brother in the seat in front of me.

I hadn't even paid attention to the fact that it was my birthday today, for a few reasons. First off, no one mentioned it to me all day, because I normally like it when my birthday isn't a big deal. Secondly, my mother was going to share with our pack, a very important decision, which was taking up most of the space in my mind.

I greeted the twins like I would have any other day I see them with a general hello.

We rode the bus the whole way home. When we got off, my siblings did what they normally do and ran up to there rooms from the side of the house and climbed in through their windows on opposite sides of our big white house in the back of the cul de sac. Speaking of which, not many places in Harrisburg, PA have a cul de sac, at least from what I noticed.

I walked up the door like I normally do and reached for the doorknob. However, before opening it, I stopped. I heard something inside, something that sounded like at least fifty steady heartbeats, I could make out each one. They were all very calm and strong. Gotta love super hearing.

I extended my claws, being extremely cautious. Normally, having dozens of people behind a door when the blinds were closed and the lights were off wasn't a good thing.

Claws still extended, I slowly opened the door. As soon as I had it open the whole way, I heard everyone inside yell.

"Surprise!" they screamed.

Before I could do anything my vision was blinded by very thick brown hair.

"Happy Birthday, my little beta." My mother whispered in my ear as she released me from her hug.

As she let me go, I looked around the room and saw fifty wolves from our pack standing around the living room. Behind my mother and to the left were Zak and Stephanie, with giant smiles on the faces. On my mother's right, was my Uncle Jack, laughing at how surprised I was. He walked up to me and patted me on the back wishing me a happy birthday.

I walked into my home, past all of my friends and family, greeting everyone. Finally, I made it to the kitchen and sat down around the table next to my brother. We started talking for a few minutes, I can't even remember about what, but after about five minutes, my mother called everyone back to the living room.

When I walked in, I noticed a huge stack of presents resting on the coffee table. This is the most that we've ever done on my birthday. I wasn't overwhelmed, but it was strange. Turning fifteen was a big deal in our pack, but I never expected this.

I made my way over to the couch, sat in between my mother and uncle, and started opening presents.

Now, most of them weren't that great. I don't want to sound unappreciative, but some were just lame; like wool socks, notebooks, my Aunt Nancy got me shoelaces for some unknown reason.

After a while though, I hit the jackpot; the things I asked for. First, from my Aunt Vanessa, Jack's wife, I received a brand new pair of steel-toed boots. I asked for these, that way when the claws on my feet grow, it'll be harder for me the rip open the ends of my shoes. Next, was from my mother; a pair of fingerless leather gloves. These were perfect for the winter months because it let me use my claws without destroying my gloves and my hands being cold. Not so useful now, because it's the end of April, but I would still wear them because they looked cool.

Finally, my last present, and it was from my Uncle Jack. I ripped it open and looked inside. It was the backpack that I wanted; a simple drawstring backpack, but when you opened it up, it had at least two dozen pockets throughout the interior. One of the pockets, however, had a giant bungle.

Slowly, so my mother, who was talking to Nancy and not paying attention, wouldn't notice, I opened the pocket and looked inside. It was was a stack of money, I couldn't tell how much it was by eyeballing it, but the bill on the outside of the stack was a hundred.

I closed the pocket and shot a look at my uncle who was on my right. He simply looked at me with a smile and said, "Don't say anything. You're welcome."

He got up, patted me on the shoulder, and walked off into the kitchen. I made a mental note to count all the money later when I was alone in my room.

Once my mother cleared away all the presents, she ushered everyone into the kitchen for cake.

I could smell it before she even brought it in. It was my favorite; chocolate cake, with strawberry icing. My mouth started watering instantly.

From then on, the party started. Everyone was spread throughout the house talking, eating cake, and kept wishing me a happy birthday. Every last wolf seemed to be having a good time, all of them except, strangely, my mother. Which was strange because she's normally the life of the party, being alpha and all.

No matter where I went, she would just keep standing in the same corner of the living room, watching me, a tear in her eye. After about an hour of this, I walked up to her.

"Is everything all right, mother?" I asked.

"Oh, I'm fine Jensen, just happy you're having a good time." She answered, wiping the tear from her eye.

"Are you sure?" I double-checked

She nodded.

"Go enjoy the party. We have to start the ceremony soon."

With that, I turned and reentered the fray of wolves in my home. I knew she was lying to me, and she wasn't all right, and even though I was her favorite, I knew better than to argue with the alpha. No one, and I mean no one, argues with the alpha.

After about another hour or so, the party died down. Everyone had had their fill of cake and chatter, and they all looked run down. My Uncle Jack had passed out in the armchair in the back corner of the living room, sleeping off the four pieces of cake he had eaten.

At this point, my mother addressed the wolves as a whole, standing on top of the couch to make sure she was heard.

"Wolves, your attention please."

Instantly, the few conversations that were going on stopped, and everyone focused on her.

"I would like for you all to go home, gather any wolves that are not here, and converge in our backyard. The ceremony will start soon."

At her words, all the wolves in my home stood up, and left, even my Uncle Jack, who had awoken at my mother's first call, had ran to his house.

2

Chapter Two: The ceremony

I ran to my room at my mother's instructions and changed into a nicer pair of clothes; a polo shirt, khakis, and dress shoes. Very rarely did I ever have to bust these out, but tonight was special.

Once I was dressed and checked myself in the mirror, I ran back downstairs and met my mother and siblings in the backyard.

When I arrived every werewolf in my pack was standing there, all had gathered within the twenty minutes it took me to get dressed and freshen up. They were all standing around in a circle that had my mother at its focal point. There were torches lit all around the circle.

My siblings and I started walking towards my mother and knelt in front of her. Once everyone had settled, my mother started to speak.

"Fellow wolves; family and friends, tonight is the night that I make the biggest decision of mine, and my children's lives."

The pack remained quiet while my mother paused.

"Tonight, I chose the alpha that will follow me in the event of my death."

I knew this day was coming, after all, that's why my birthday this year was such a big deal. After all the training my mother would have me do with her every day after school and on the weekends, the special attention she showed me, and how she seemed to prefer me over my siblings. It was finally time for her to name me her new second in command, the new delta, next in line to be alpha.

My mother continued her speech.

"I have recalled the sentinels, that patrol the perimeter of our town, and stopped all activity for the night, as to make sure as many wolves as possible know my decision."

I held my breath, my heart racing. It was finally time.

My mind seemed to drift for a few moments during another pause, back to a training day with my mother on a rainy Saturday morning towards the end of fall, about five years ago. I had just emerged from the forest behind our house and met my mother. Drenched to the bone in rain, I dragged the deer I had hunted to her feet. Out of breath, and stowing my claws and fangs, I had looked at my mother for approval.

She had looked down and smiled.

"My little beta, you've done a wonderful job." She said, as she picked up the deer and heaved it onto her shoulder.

"One day," she continued, "You'll understand why I am so much harder on you than your brother and sister. One day, everything will all make sense."

At the time, I had no idea what she meant. However, now, it all made sense. At least, I thought it did.

"After thinking this over for a very, very long time, and considering every single last option at my disposal, I have chosen." My mother continued.

I got ready to stand, sure it was going to be me.

"My delta, second in command, and next alpha…" She let the last word ring out for a few moments.

I started smiling.

"Will be…" I started to stand. "Jackson, my brother."

I stopped. It had felt like someone had punched me in the chest with all of their might. Confused, I was no longer paying attention to anything going on around me. Vaguely, I was aware that my uncle had joined my mother in front of me, but my head was still down, and I was still kneeling.

How could she not have picked me? Why did she pick Jack? Yes, he was her brother. Yes, he was an extremely powerful wolf, but he was fifteen years older than her. Even with us being werewolves and having extended lives, there was a very good chance that he would die before her anyway, and she would end up having to select another delta anyway. Why not pick someone just as strong, maybe stronger, but much younger and ready to shoulder the burden? Why not pick me?

All of these thoughts came racing through my head for about a second before I received a jab with an elbow in my side. Zak, who was on my left, was looking at me with very harsh eyes. I snapped back to reality.

The ceremony was ending, and my brother and sister started to stand. My mother began to speak once again.

"Now, my children, to christen Jack as the new delta of the pack, please, howl with me."

With that, my siblings and I, along with my mother and uncle, howled at the moon. Slowly, all of the wolves around the perimeter joined in, their eyes glowing white; the normal color of a beta. My mother's eyes shone red; the color of an alpha, Jacks, slowly but surely, glowed white but changed to a solid orange; the color of a delta. The only outlier in the colors of eyes around the backyard was mine. For some reason, ever since I was born, my eyes always glowed with a very bright sky blue color.

After a few more moments of howling, everyone had stopped. My mother had dispersed the ceremony, and the wolves were now starting to leave. Uncle Jack was among the last to leave, due to now having a responsibility, like my mother, to make sure that everyone was seen off.

Before my mother could stop me, and before the backyard had even cleared out, I ran into the house through the back door, climbed the stairs and entered my room, slamming the door behind me out of anger.

I ran around my room like a madman. Never in my life, had I been this angry and confused.

During my rage, I turned around and noticed that my door had split in half from slamming it. I made a mental note to fix it later.

With a sigh, I flopped down and sat on my bed, trying to clear my head.

She's the alpha. I thought she knows what she's doing. I can't be too mad.

This thought did help a little. I was still extremely irritated, but I figured I'd work through it.

A few moments later, my mother knocked on the remains of my door.

"May I come in?" She asked, cracking the door.

I simply nodded.

My mother entered my room and took a spot on the bed next to me. She placed a comforting arm around my shoulders, even though I didn't want it.

"I know it's hard right now, Jensen, to understand my decision. But believe me, it was the best one."

I looked down at the ground, refusing to make eye contact as she continued.

"You have a very bright and difficult future ahead of you, little beta. You don't even begin to realize how important you are to our pack; to our family."

I nodded, still upset.

"I'll leave you be for now." my mother offered. "I'll wake you first thing in the morning. We must resume your training, having missed this afternoon."

I nodded once more. My mother squeezed me, removed her arm from my shoulders, and started walking out of my room. As she opened the door, she looked back at me.

"I love you, little one."

I waited a few seconds before responding.

"Love you too."

I looked up and saw my mother smile while she closed the door behind her.

After sitting there for a few more minutes, a thought returned to me. I had never counted the money Uncle Jack had given me.

I jumped up and grabbed my new bag. I opened it up, unzipped the flap, and took out the huge stack of money that was inside.

Having to count it multiple times, because I couldn't believe how much it was, I had figured out my uncle had given me two thousand dollars, all in hundreds. My mind was blank; I had been so mad at him earlier for taking what I thought was my place as Delta, and he did something as generous as this. I made another mental note to apologize to him tomorrow.

Looking over at the clock, I noticed that it was eleven o'clock at night. Normally, I wouldn't have been tired. Because I'm a werewolf, I can generally stay awake for days on end. This is because my brain will just heal itself instead of misfiring and causing hallucinations and whatnot. However, tonight I was drained.

Laying down in my bed, I quickly drifted off to sleep, mentally preparing myself for the training I was going to partake in the morning.

3

Chapter Three: The chase

This is where things start getting weird, so stick with me.

Normally, at night, I dream. Most of the time I don't remember them, but I still have the feeling that I had a dream. On nights that I don't, like on this night, bad things always happen. It's sort of like a premonition, but instead of seeing something, it's just a feeling I get, because of things that have happened. Maybe I should explain a little more.

There have been five nights in my life where I haven't dreamt. The first was when I was about nine years old, and I was awoken in the early hours of the morning. My house was on fire, and my mother was rushing me out. We managed to put it out in about an hour, but there was still a lot of damage.

The next time was about a year later, my pack was being attacked in the middle of the night by a rival pack from a few miles away. We fought for hours and lost a lot of wolves. It took us weeks to repair all of the homes. Not good.

You get the point. No dreams mean bad news.

I woke up to my mother shaking me, saying something that took me a few moments to make out.

"Wake up, Jensen. Wake up now!" She sounded alarmed.

"Wha-" I sat bolt upright.

I heard what was making her act this way. When I turned and looked at her, she had a horror-struck look on her face. There was a very deep howl coming from about a two miles away.

"What is that?" I asked, pulling my covers off and kicking my legs over the bed.

"No time to explain now, little beta. Get dressed. Pack a bag. Meet me in the backyard in five minutes. Hurry!" she said all of this quickly.

My mother got up and walked out of my room without any further explanation. I decided I better do as I'm told, no one disobeys a direct order from the alpha.

I ran around my room gathering my things. First, I put on some clothes, just a regular T-shirt, jeans, my new boots, and my new gloves. Grabbing the backpack my uncle gave me for my birthday, I put a few changes of clothes inside. Quickly, I ran downstairs and out the back door in the kitchen.

My mother was standing at the edge of the forest, waiting for me. She still looked terrified.

"I'm ready," I told her.

"Now listen to me, Jensen. We need to run, as fast as possible. Stay close to me, but slightly behind. Keep all of your senses on high alert. If you hear anything strange, you tell me immediately." She gave these orders quickly, but I nodded in agreement.

"Okay." She said. "Stay close."

With those words, my mother shifted. Her eyes glowed blood red, her claws and fangs elongated, the hair on her arms and head grew and thickened. As my mother began to change, so did I. Everything that was happening to her was also happening to me, except my eyes glowed sky blue, instead of red.

After a few seconds, our shifts were completed. My mother took a whiff of the air, and her eyes became wide; panicky. I could hear her heart rate increase.

"Let's go." She said and started running through the forest.

I followed her just as she instructed. Very quickly, we had reached top speed. Well, I should say, my mother, did. I had to hold back just a bit, because for some reason, whenever I went all out, I was even faster than my mother. It was like the wind would bend around me, and let me go faster, making me more aerodynamic.

Anyway, at around three hundred miles an hour, we were quickly out of the forest. We passed houses, towns, more forests. Everything was blazing past us as we ran.

As we ran, now and then I would hear a faint roar or howl, and caught a whiff of something that was burning. Distinctive burning. Whenever I noticed something like this, I shared it with my mother. Every time she would yell back, "It's still far away, just keep going." So that's what I did.

My mother did not stop running until we reached a sign on the right side of the road. It said we were in Hollidaysburg, Pennsylvania. We were a good one hundred and twenty miles away. Not bad considering it only took us about twenty minutes or so. I turned to my mother, she was catching her breath, which is weird because she normally had great stamina.

"So, where to now, mother?" I asked.

"Just a little further up the road." She gasped. The same howl I heard before echoed in the distance. It was getting closer now. How was it able to keep up?

"Let's go." My mother said and started running again. I followed.

We ran a little farther down the road, about five miles. My mother turned left, into another forest, and I, naturally, followed.

As we ran my mother was swiping her claws left and right, cutting down trees, trying to slow down whatever was chasing us. I followed her lead, moved a few yards to the left, and chopped down sections of trees on my own. I'm happy that our claws can cut through almost everything like it's butter, and are nearly indestructible.

My mother stopped about two miles into this forest, coming out of her shift. About two hundred feet in front of us, there was a clearing, fifty feet in diameter, in a perfect circle. It looked normal enough, except there was a funny haze over the entrance to the clearing, like heat coming off of blacktop on a hot summer day. I tried to narrow my eyes, kicking in my infrared and night visions but I still couldn't see through it.

"What's in that clearing?" I asked my mother while moving forward.

It took her a few moments to answer.

"Jensen, please, we have enough time. I think it's time I explained everything." Her voice was breaking like she was about to start crying.

I turned around and looked at her, and she did, indeed, have tears in her eyes. Immediately, I stopped walking, concerned. There was a tree stump a few feet to my right, so I sat down.

"First off, where are we?" I asked.

"Canoe Creek. It's a park. Just outside of Hollidaysburg."

I nodded.

"Jensen, I need to be honest with you about everything. Why we're here, what we're doing, where you're going." I interrupted her, by the way, never a good idea to interrupt an alpha.

"What do you mean, where I'm going?"

She didn't seem mad.

"In time. Because I'm also going to tell you about your father."

This was unbelievable. My mother never talked about my father. Not once, in my fifteen years of life. Why now? What was going on? I decided to wait, and let my mother regain her thoughts and continue speaking.

"Jensen, your father was a very, very powerful man. He was smart, handsome, kind; the kindest person I have ever met in my life. We had a wonderful time together."

I sat in silence while she took a breath, more tears coming to her eyes.

"Have you ever wondered, Jensen, why I always took interest in you? Why I showed you more than your brother and sister? Have you ever wondered why your eyes and claws are different colors than the rest of the pack?"

"Yes," I answered.

"I figured as much, little beta. Jensen, the reason I put you to a higher standard, the reason I didn't choose you to be Delta, is because of your father. I know you wouldn't be able to be around, I didn't know it would be so soon, but I knew you'd be gone."

She took another pause, steadying herself.

"What are you talking about? Where am I going?"

"This is all about your father, and who you are. Jensen, do you remember all of
    those stories about heroes in ancient Greece?"

I nodded. I knew that the original immortal wolves were from ancient

Greece. That's where all the werewolves started.

My mother continued.

"Well, they're all true. All of those gods and heroes exist or did exist, for some of them. Your father told me all about it."

I was confused.

"Wait, how could my father have told you all of this? Was he a historian or something?"

She took a very deep breath.

"No Jensen, your father, is much more than a historian. He created us."

"What?" I was really confused now.

"Little one, your father is Zeus. God of the sky. King of Olympus."

4

Chapter Four: A fight for our lives

"What?" I said again, weakly.

My mother never talked about my father. Not once. Now she tells me he's an ancient Greek god, and not just any god, but the king of all gods. What was she thinking? Did she go insane?

"Yes, Jensen. Zeus, king of all gods, god of lightning, is your father."

I sat and thought about it for a little while. My eyes, glowing sky blue, I extended my claws and looked down at them, examining every detail. They were a bronze color. Most werewolves' claws were just dark brown. I've noticed both of these things before, but I never thought that this would be the answer to my questions. It finally made sense why my mother never talked about him.

From what I read in myths and books about my ancestor, Lycaon, I learned he was the first werewolf. In my research, I read that the gods had all agreed to never, ever have children with a werewolf. The reason why is because Zeus had created Lycaon.

The story goes that Zeus was invited to Lycaon's mansion in Arcadia. Being the king of Arcadia, he wanted to treat the king of Olympus to a great feast. When he served the meal, Zeus didn't eat a bite. Lycaon attempted to serve him a cooked child named Nyctimus, Lycaons own son. I guess he was trying to prove that Zeus wasn't omniscient. He was wrong, Zeus caught on immediately and turned Lycaon and all fifty of his remaining sons into the first-ever werewolves; the originals, the immortals.

Eventually, the werewolves evolved a little more and became like me. No one has ever seen an immortal in over one hundred years. However, my mother and I are direct descendants of Lycaon himself, and the first-ever female werewolf. Normally, women don't survive the bite, but somehow she did, and she and Lycaon had children. Those children had children, and eventually, they evolved into what I am.

At last, my entire life made sense. I always knew my siblings and I had different dads, but I never would have thought that my dad was a god.

"That's why we're here." My mother said after a few moments.

"What?" I asked, snapping back to reality.

"The thing that's chasing us, Jensen, is a monster from the Underworld. I heard it off in the distance, and realized it was coming for you."

I remembered the burning smell, and the howls I heard while we were running. What was it?

"I brought you here so you could be safe Jensen, even if it means I don't see you for a long time."

"What is it that was following us?"

My mother took a sniff in the air. Her face turned chalk white, full of panic. She stood up and grabbed my hand.

"I'll explain while we run. Quick, to that clearing!"

I caught a whiff of what my mother had smelt. It was an acrid smoke, like burning flesh. In the distance, I heard a very loud howl, maybe about a mile away. My mother dragged me off towards the clearing.

"The thing that's chasing us normally travels in a pack." My mother was saying.

"But what is it?" I asked again, needing an answer. "I can't fight something if I have no idea what it is."

However, just as we entered the edge of the clearing, my mother didn't have to answer. From our left, the trees broke and a gigantic dog, that looked like a rottweiler, stood in front of us.

"Hellhound." My mother whispered, extending an arm out in front of me.

The huge rottweiler had red and black striped fur, trash can lid sized paws, and teeth that were sharper than knives. Where the red stripes in its fur were, you could see fire and embers flying off of them like mini fireworks. The smoke smell was even stronger now that the hellhound was up close; almost overpowering.

My mother was looking around the clearing, possibly keeping an eye out for the rest of the pack. I tuned my ears, trying to pick up any sounds of oncoming attackers. Nothing, maybe it was on its own, or the pack was very far behind. Either way, I didn't want to find out.

"Fight hard. Get past it. Go to the temple." My mother ordered.

"What temple?" I questioned.

Before she could answer, the haze that was hanging around the clearing started to clear. Behind the hellhound, a magnificent marble white temple was erected. For some reason, I hadn't seen it before. It was covered with lightning bolts and clouds that were engraved into the marble columns.

At the very top of the front wall, there was a statue of what I assumed to be Zeus. He wore a Greek tunic, a thunderbolt in his left hand, and his classic shoulder-length hair and bushy beard. The statue and temple seemed to radiate power. It was kind of intimidating.

I nodded to my mother, as we both shifted. We weren't going to go out without a fight.

Real quick, I should explain one thing. When an alpha werewolf roars, it's probably one of the most intimidating and terror-striking things you could ever hear. Every animal that heard it slithered away. As my mother did it now, however, the hellhound didn't even flinch. I think, maybe, it smirked. If that was possible. Not good.

The hellhound pounced, fangs bared. My mother and I dodged, me going to the right, she to the left. However, my mother wasn't quite quick enough, and one of the hellhounds fangs caught her arm. I heard her scream in pain and turned around. From where the fang had caught her arm, smoke was starting to rise. With my eyes in full shift, I could vaguely see the wound trying to heal, just to be ripped open again.

My mother ripped a part of her shirt off and tied it around the wound. She looked at the hellhound, madder than anything.

I charged at the right flank of the beast, claws bared. As best as I could I sank my claws into the hellhound's side. My hand went knuckle deep. When I pulled it out, my hand was covered in bright red blood. The beast slammed me away with its massive paw. Flying back, I slammed into a nearby tree. A little dazed, I stood up, ready to fight.

Extremely quickly, my mother slid under the hellhound, raking her claws against its stomach. I could see that it did damage, but not as much as my strike, which I thought was strange.

However, even though my mother was quick, again, she wasn't quick enough. Before she could get away, the hellhound pinned her against the ground with its paw. Two of its claws sank into each of my mother's shoulders. She screamed in pain as smoke started to billow from the holes. The longer that the claws stayed in, the thicker the smoke came out.

I ran as fast as I could to her aid. With all of my strength, which was a lot, I slammed into the side of the hellhound. It flew at least forty feet into the forest, taking out large areas of trees as it went. Considering as it was about twenty-five feet tall and ten feet long, I wasn't surprised.

Kneeling next to my mother, I looked at her wounds. I removed her bandage from her arm and saw that it was finally starting to heal over. Her shoulders, however, were extremely bad. Blood was pouring out of them like a river. Thinking and working as fast as possible, I grabbed her hand, silently willing her pain to seep out of her and into me. This was something that werewolves could do, however, if used too much, it could kill us.

It hurt worse than anything that I've ever experienced. Thankfully though, I could see the wounds closing rapidly. Without the pain weighing down her senses, my mother's body was able to focus on healing.

When I let go, my mother moved into a kneeling position next to me. I could hear the hellhound getting up in the distance.

"Get to the temple, now. I'll hold it off." My mother ordered me.

"No," I told her. "I'm staying, or you're coming with me."

Bad idea.

"Do not disobey me." She commanded softly, a growl in her voice.

The argument was over. Whether she was my mother or not, she was still the alpha.

I helped her to her feet, and once she was stable, she started to run to the doors of the temple. They were made of solid oak and looked like they could withstand a full force tornado. As soon as I reached them, however, it happened.

My mother screamed like someone was about to chop off her head. A blood churning scream. I spun around just in time to see it happen.

The hellhound had jumped out of the woods. My mother wasn't expecting it, and the creature had caught her, right in its mouth. It's knife-like fangs piercing my mother's body. Flames were flying out of the puncture holes. That's when I lost it.

My vision went black, and I only remember bits and pieces. I remember running as fast as I could, claws out. I was in the air after a massive leap, but nothing was holding me up, it was like I was standing on an invisible platform. There was a smell like ozone, and then I was on the ground.

I came around a few moments later. Very light-headed and dizzy. My mother was laying on the ground next to me, blood coming out of her chest and stomach. Even though I felt like I had just gotten thrown a mile down the road, I knelt next to her and took her pain again.

It took longer this time, probably because of the severity of the wounds, but after about five minutes, her wounds were healed. She woke up a few seconds later.

"What happened?" She asked, coming out of her shift.

"I don't remember," I told her. I stood up uneasily and explained the bits that were fresh in my mind.

She considered this for a few moments before she spoke.

"You need to get inside, quick. You'll be safe in there. If any more hellhounds come around, they won't be able to get in. Wait for your vanguard. They should be here in a few hours."

"What vanguard? What do you mean?" I was starting to get confused again.

"Just trust me, Jensen." She said as she struggled to her feet. "I need to get back home. You'll be safe from here." She hugged me.

I didn't argue, she knew what was best. However, I didn't want her to leave.

When she let go of me, she didn't say another word. All she did was start running out of the woods, back home. When she was out of view, I turned around and faced the door of the temple.

Slowly, I walked forward. I pushed on the solid oak doors, which were a lot lighter than what they seemed. As I entered the temple, the interior took my breath away. It was stunning for what it was.

There were more marble columns with lightning bolts engraved into them. Statues of Zeus were standing in between each of the six columns. The walls were covered with paintings of the god. One was Zeus and two other men; on Zeus' right a man in black robes and long black hair, his eyes looked empty, on Zeus' left a man that looked like he spent all day on a boat that was out at sea: Zeus brothers; Hades and Poseidon.

At the far end of the temple, there was a brazier that, upon me entering the temple, ignited on its own accord. That was pretty cool. Around the brazier, was a bench. I walked over and sat down, taking in everything that happened today.

My mother and I being attacked, finding out that my father is Zeus (somehow), I was passed over for Delta and the position went to my uncle. How much more could happen in one day? Well, little did I know, a lot more.

Now and then I checked my watch, slowly seeing the time pass by. When I walked into the temple it was four o'clock in the morning. Now, it was only going on six, but I felt like I was sitting there, waiting for this so-called vanguard to take me somewhere by my guess, for days.

After a while, checking my watch it was around seven, and the sun was coming up, I was about to call it quits and head home, regardless of what my mother said. Just as I was picking up my bag and slinging it over my shoulder, I heard heartbeats outside. By my count, there were about five of them.

My mind worked fast. The five heartbeats were strong and steady, like warriors. Whether these were more hellhounds, or something else, I wasn't sure.

I took up a post behind a statue of Zeus that was big enough to hide me. Silently, I extend my claws, just in case there was another attack. The heartbeats were getting closer and closer. After about a minute of waiting,

I saw shadows moving underneath the door thanks to the light from the brazier. Seconds later, the doors opened slowly, revealing five people, all covered head to toe in what seemed to be ancient Greek armor.

Watching closely, I saw them enter. In the lead was a guy of average height, African-American, with a short military-style haircut. On his left was a girl that was a bit shorter, with long black hair tied up in a ponytail. Behind her was another guy the blonde hair, but a little longer, about to his shoulders. To his right, there was a red-headed girl, a bow drawn. Finally, at the back of the group, with shield and sword drawn, was a girl with piercing sea-green eyes, and long brown hair braided down her back. Taking a whiff of the air, I caught the scent of strawberries.

Everyone had weapons drawn like they were ready for a fight. The front two had shields out, and spears pointing through. After looking around for a few moments, the girl in the back started speaking.

"Jensen Smith? I know you're here. Please come out." Her voice sounded nice but strong.

I listened to their heartbeats. All steady; they were all calm. However, I didn't move, still unsure if I could trust them.

"We're here to help Jensen. Please." The girl said this time she sounded a little irritated. Her heartbeat didn't change at all, she was telling the truth.

I stepped out from behind my hiding place, claws still extended but hidden behind my back.

"Who are you?" I asked.

The girl in the front with the black hair answered.

"Jensen Smith?" She was extremely cheery and lowered her weapons, walking up to me, arm extended for a handshake. "My name's Rachael Sage, daughter of Athena. Goddess of wisdom and warfare."

I took her hand, stowing my claws quickly while I did so. She seemed nice enough. When I let go, she sheathed her sword. Did she say her mom was a goddess?

"Who are the rest of you?" I asked, addressing everyone else.

The girl named Rachael was the one who answered.

"Well, first up is Blake Albern, he's a son of Ares. God of war." She pointed to the African-American kid in the front, he raised a hand in greeting. "Next, is Robert Brantley, but everyone calls him Rob. He's a son of Hephaestus. Our blacksmith." Rob gave me a big smile.

"I'm Penelope. Penelope Conway. Daughter of Poseidon. God of the sea." The girl with braided hair said, cutting Rachael off before she could start. The way she spoke, it sounded like she was mad but very commanding. Why she was mad, I had no idea.

Rachael cleared her throat and started talking again.

"That's Megan Bard, daughter of Apollo. God of archery, and well, a lot of stuff." Megan had moved over to the window next to the door, bow still drawn, not looking at anyone. "She's really shy, but once you get to know her, she's the sweetest," Rachael whispered to me.

I nodded. This was strange, all of these kids showing up here, out of nowhere, all of the kids of gods. I walked back over the brazier and sat down.

"We're going to camp here for now," Penelope was saying. "Rest up a few hours, then we need to head back. Blake, you're on the first watch."

Everyone, minus Blake and Megan, came and sat around the brazier as well. They weren't talking, and I was collecting my thoughts, trying to figure out what question I had first. Rachael started cooking eggs and bacon over the fire. The son of Ares took a post next to the door, but able to see out a window.

"So, why are you guys here?" I asked, after about ten minutes of silence.

"We're here to take you to a school, Jensen. It's a school for people like us; demigods." Penelope answered.

"Okay. Why didn't my mother take me to this so-called school? I feel sure she and I would have been able to make it on our own." I still didn't trust these people, but most of them seemed okay, and they were the only people that could answer my questions.

"You're mother, since she isn't a demigod, isn't able to get past the school's protection. Only people and things from our world can enter." Rachael told me.

It also occurred to me that my mother and I had almost gotten killed by just one hellhound. I decided not to share that quite yet.

"Fair enough," I said. "What do you do at this school?"

"We train," Rob started, "to fight monsters, hone our abilities, use our powers." He was working with a few pieces of metal, his hands were moving extremely fast, making some sort of device.

"What powers? What abilities?" That didn't make sense, besides my werewolf abilities, I didn't have anything special.

"Well, Jensen, since my mother is Athena, I have extreme wisdom and intelligence. I also can make battle plans." Rachael started explaining. "Rob and all of his siblings can do very high scale blacksmithing."

I looked over at Penelope.

"What about you?"

She stared daggers at me.

"I'm one of the select few of Poseidon's children that has the power, not only to breath underwater, as all of my siblings have, but I can also control water currents and water as a whole."

I nodded, kind of impressed. That was a cool ability.

"She's being modest." Rachael continued. "She can also tell you exactly where you are, anywhere in the ocean. Not all children of Poseidon can do that."

"What about the other two?" I asked, nodding to Blake and Megan.

"Blake," Rachael said. "Has the innate ability to use any weapon he comes across. Also, he's a very, very good battle tactician, like all children of Ares. Megan is an expert marksman with a bow. She can also heal just about any wound. Her music isn't bad either."

I remembered reading something about Apollo, Megan's father. Not only was he the god of archery, but he was also the god of poetry, music, medicine, and oracles. There were others included too, but I couldn't remember them all.

Those were all pretty impressive things. I started to wonder if I had any special powers, being a son of Zeus.

After hearing Rachael and Penelope explain some things, I started to believe them. This temple that we were sitting in wasn't here for no reason. People had worshiped the gods, and what if they were real? I glanced over at Rob's hands again. He stopped playing with the metal in his hands, and it was now a fully functioning watch. How had he made that so quickly?

Rachael started handing out the finished eggs and bacon. She extended some to me, and I took it with a word of thanks. I hadn't realized how hungry I was after everything that happened today. After just a few seconds, my food was gone.

"When do you want to leave Penny?" Rob asked, making a few finishing touches on his watch.

"Penny?" I laughed.

"Only my friends call me that, son of Zeus." She snapped back at me. She addressed Rob. "We'll rest here for another hour, then pack up and head back to the school. With lightning boy here, we'll probably have to slow down."

Seriously, what was her problem with me?

"Don't go slow on my account. I can keep up, trust me." I said bluntly.

Did they not know I was a werewolf? Probably not, most werewolves were pretty secretive, my pack included. She thought I couldn't keep up? Did she think that I was just some random demigod that was dropped into the middle of a forest? Whatever she thought, I was gonna prove her wrong.

I decided not to let them know I was a werewolf yet. Penelope already didn't like me, and I didn't want to push it, just in case someone had a prejudice against werewolves. The few people in my life that I met who knew about werewolves and the misconception that we were all murders.

We sat there for another hour. Rachael chatting with me about all the great things at the school. She mentioned that there hasn't been a child of Zeus there in almost twenty years. Not that Zeus stopped having kids with mortals, but because the ones they tried to recruit never wanted to come. I found this weird but didn't question it. Even though I was curious as to how many brothers and sisters I had out there.

"So, typically, what powers do children of Zeus have?" I asked her.

"Well, normally, from what I've been told, they either have the power to control wind currents, or redirect lightning. There was a story once, of a son of Zeus that was chosen by the god himself to have both abilities, and he could generate lightning on his own, without having to utilize the sky itself.

But, that demigod died hundreds of years ago, and no one has had that power since."

"So chances are that I'll be able to fly or summon lightning from the sky. That's pretty cool, I guess." I was still a bit skeptical.

"Let's get going," Penelope said, getting up from her spot on the bench.

Rob got up as well, tossing me the watch he had been working on.

"Figured you wouldn't have any weapons, so I whipped this up for you. If we get attacked, press the button."

"Thanks," I said, slightly confused, examining the watch.

There was a button on the side, where the dial would normally be. I didn't know what it was supposed to do, so I didn't touch it quite yet.

After everyone had packed up, Penelope took the lead and walked out of the oak doors. Little did I know, that I was about to see a whole new world.

5

Chapter Five: First day of school

Penelope set everyone up in guard positions. Blake and Rob were in the front, swords, and shields drawn. Rachael was on my left, Penelope on the right. Behind us all, with her bow in hand, was Megan.

We walked for a very long time. Rachael kept eyeballing me, and jumped and blushed every time I talked to her.

Not a whole lot happened as we walked for the first few hours. Rachael was explaining to me how the school works in more detail.

"Every god has a dorm. We live there with our siblings."

"Okay. Now, you said there are no other children of Zeus at the school, so I get an entire dorm to myself?" I asked.

"Yup. The major three gods; Zeus, Poseidon, and Hades, are all on the top floors." She explained.

"Is there anyone in those beside Penelope?"

"She has a couple of siblings there, only about ten. No one is in Hades, it's sort of honorary because he's one of Kronos' sons, but no children of Hades ever come to school."

I nodded, it was nice that someone was explaining things to me.

"Why don't children of Hades ever show up?" I asked.

"Well, I can't say for sure, but I think it's because most of them are loners. Hades himself separates from Olympus because he doesn't have a seat on Mount Olympus."

Again, I nodded, at a loss for words.

"There's a dorm for every major god, and some of the minor ones, like Hecate; goddess of magic and crossroads." Rachael continued.

"What happens if a dorm gets overfilled?" I wondered.

"No idea," Rachael answered. "It's never happened."

"I wonder what the training consists of." I pondered, looking around, keeping my senses on high alert.

"Oh, lots of sword fighting, defense, power control. It's a lot of fun." Rob chimed in from in front of me.

"Who's going to teach me how to use my powers?" I asked the group as a whole.

Blake is the one who answered.

"Probably Leonardo or Marchessa."

"Who are they?"

"Headmaster and mistress of the school. Leo's a son of Athena, my much older brother. Marchessa is a daughter of Ares." Rachael said.

"What if they don't know what kind of powers I have?" I asked, kind of concerned.

"Well, as I explained earlier, all children of Zeus have either control over wind or lightning and some have control over both. Generally, your powers will emerge soon if they haven't already. Sometimes, the gods chose which powers you get, and they let Leo know so he can tell you."

"How long have you all been at the school?" I asked the group.

"Five years for me. Blake, about seven. Megan's been there for, what?" She looked back at Megan. "Six?" Megan nodded.

"I've been there for eight." Rob boasted. "Second longest of anyone there, besides Penny. She's been there for ten."

"You've been there since you were five?" I was shocked, how could someone start training to fight that young?

"Not important." She snapped.

I shrugged and started processing all the information I was given.

Before I could ask any more questions, however, Penelope stopped us dead in our tracks, looking off to her right.

"Quiet." She ordered in a whisper. I gathered since she was one of the most experienced, and a child of Poseidon, she was usually in charge.

I heard what she had, surprised that she caught it before me. There was a rustling in the tree line to our right. Everyone adjusted their position toward the noise. No one but me reacted.

As everyone was getting set up, something jumped from the tree line. Blake and Rob were still in front of me but hadn't expected the attack. Quick as I could, I pushed them out of the way, and dodged myself, jumping backward.

Before I knew what was happening, one more enemy jumped from the tree line. I moved out of the way, and it landed where I was standing. Rob and Blake jumped up, shields raised.

The monsters in front of us were the weirdest things I've ever seen. They looked more or less normal from the waist up until you got to their heads; which were covered with snakes and sported tusks. From the waist down, they had snake-like trunks instead of legs. They would have been beautiful women, if it weren't for, ya know, everything about them.

"Gorgons!" Rachael yelled.

I heard the myths about gorgons from school. There were three sisters; Medusa, Stheno, and Euryale. Medusa's stare could turn any person or animal to stone. Stheno had a bloodlust that was never quenched and was constantly murdering. Euryale had a scream that would cause her enemies to drop dead if caught in the soundwave. Three extremely dangerous ladies; and two of them were standing in front of us.

The gorgons attacked again, this time charging Penelope and Rachael. They both dodged, and Rachael landed at my side. I looked around for Megan and didn't see her anywhere.

"Don't worry about her," Rachael said as if reading my mind. "She's trying to find a good vantage point."

"So which one is which?" I asked. "I'm assuming Medusa isn't here since none of us are stone."

The Gorgons were standing about twenty feet in front of us, brandishing their claws, wings sprouted from their back. I couldn't tell the difference except for the one on the right had longer tusks.

"The one on the left is Euryale, keep out of the way if she screams, it won't end well. The one on the right is Stheno, she'll try everything to kill us."

"Wonder who I made mad to send the gorgons after us." I pondered.

"No idea, but the gorgons don't just show up out of nowhere."

At this point, the conversation couldn't continue; the Gorgons were charging again. Stheno pulled two daggers from behind her back and slashed at Rachael and I. Euryale turned toward Rob, Blake, and now Penelope, who had rolled next to them during her dodge. There was a sound like a jet engine.

I pushed Rachael out of the way to avoid Stheno's blades, at the same time I jumped over to where Rob, Blake, and Penelope were standing. Remembering my watch, and what Rob had told me, I pressed the button as I went.

Thankfully, I was just quick enough. I stood in front of the three of them, but instead of being shattered to bits from a sonic blast, I was protected by a shield. Where my watch used to be, there was a magnificent bronze shield, about five feet in diameter. There was a sound like a gong that had gotten hit by the world's biggest mallet, but everyone was safe.

I brought the shield down to my side and looked at the gorgons; a smile on my face.

"Let's do this," I told them and charged.

I made my way toward Euryale since she was closer. Her sister charged at my vanguard behind me, which now consisted of everyone but Megan. They had all raised their shields to fend off the attacker, but Stheno was too quick. She slipped under Rob's shield and sank her dagger up to the hilt in between his ribs. Penelope swiped with her sword, but Stheno ducked under it.

Quick as I could, I swiped at Euryale with my shield, remembering I had no weapons. She dodged it and took a swing with her claws. They caught me in the chest, and it hurt, but I could feel the wounds healing quickly. A few seconds later, there was no sign of the cuts except for the slashes in my shirt. Behind me, I head Rachael yell.

I kicked Euryale in the chest, sending her flying, and spun around to see Stheno's other dagger pointing out of Rachael's shoulder. My vanguard was getting beaten. Running back at Stheno, I shifted. I heard an arrow fly past my head, and heard Euryale scream in pain. Megan was posted up in a tree about seventy-five feet away, letting arrows fly in Euryale's direction, and with each one, there was a cry of pain behind me.

When I got to Stheno, she looked at me, fear now in her eyes. Using the shield I still had out, I pushed everyone out of the way and threw the shield to my side. Spinning around, I sank my claws knuckle deep into Stheno's ribs; she looked shocked.

"How-" She hissed. "We were told that you were just a son of Zeus." The s in Zeus seemed to ring out for a few seconds.

"Guess whoever sent you should have warned you about werewolves." I laughed.

Before she could react, I withdrew my claws from her torso and sank my fangs into her neck. I felt something hot in my mouth, and a few moments later, I saw Stheno the gorgon burst into flames. Is that how monsters died?

"Stheno!" Euryale cried from behind me.

I spun around and saw the gorgon coming at me, arrows sticking out of her torso like porcupine quills. She jumped and sank her claws into my shoulders. She inhaled for a scream, but I kicked her in the chest again and sent her flying.

She hit the ground with a deep thud, but was instantly back on her feet, well, trunk. As the gorgon slithered toward me, I jumped in the air and landed behind her. Euryale spun around and let out a scream, but I managed to dodge. Where I was standing was now a crater ten feet in diameter.

The wounds in my shoulders had healed already. However, the Gorgon didn't look deterred. She lunged at me and sank her claws into my chest. Pain flared. If she would have been a few inches to the right, my heart would have been impaled.

Before the monster could move, I returned the favor. My claws sank into her chest, but I hit my mark.

"I will get you for this, Jensen Smith." She hissed, literally.

"I'd like to see you try," I told her, and with a little force, I ripped her in half, flames churning from the monster's corpse.

I turned around to my vanguard and noticed they were all looking at me, mouths wide open, except for Rob and Rachael, who had looks of pain on their faces.

"You're a werewolf?" Blake asked.

I shifted back to normal.

"Um, yeah, I am," I answered.

"That's cool," Rob muttered. "But, I'm kind of bleeding out here."

Megan came running up from behind me, medical bag in hand and got to work on Rob and Rachael's wounds. After a few minutes, Rob and Rachael looked almost good as new; well at least Rob was able to talk normally and start freaking out.

"Dude, I can't believe that you're a werewolf. That's seriously awesome!" He said.

"Why didn't you tell us?" Rachael asked, a twinkle in her eyes.

"Well, no offense, but I didn't trust you guys. Plus, I didn't know if you guys had any prejudice against werewolves or anything."

"Of course not!" Rachael exclaimed. "Heck, Penelope's first boyfriend was a werewolf. Right, Penny?" She turned toward her friend.

"Yeah. He was." She said, a tear in her eyes; she turned away from the rest of the group.

"Oh, yeah, I'm sorry Penny," Rachael said, patting Penelope on the arm.

"Pack everything up," Penelope ordered, wiping a tear from her eye. "We need to move. There may be more monsters coming."

That more or less put the conversation to bed.

As we started moving, everyone, not just Rachael, started to talk to me more. Rachael explained to me that she and Penny were best friends, and she felt bad that she had misspoken as she did.

"What happened? Did they have a bad break-up?" I asked her.

"Penny should be the one to tell you. It's not my place." She explained, and I let it drop. "However, just be careful. Zeus and Poseidon have a long rivalry going back to ancient times. Sometimes, their children are absorbed by it." I added this to the notepad in my head.

Rob started telling me about a motorcycle he was building back at school. It was plated with bronze, which was normally deadly to monsters, and had a bunch of different weapons and modifications. It sounded pretty cool.

"Can't wait to see it," I told him.

"Oh, it's not done yet, but give me another couple of weeks, and it'll be in fighting shape." He said with a smirk.

Blake started telling me about all the weapons they had at school; spears, swords, javelins, bows, slings, daggers, giant crossbows that were set up around the walls of the school. It all sounded pretty amazing. He told me that he would most likely be the one training me with the weapons since he was the head of the Ares dorm. I was okay with this.

Even Megan was chiming in on the conversation now and then. Apparently, according to her, every person in my vanguard was the head of their respective dorms. Megan explained some demigod medical things to me. They had this thing called ambrosia. Normally, it was eaten by the gods as regular food, but for demigods, if eaten in small quantities, it was able to heal minor injuries.

"Like ambrosia and nectar from Olympus?" I asked, remembering them from some research I had done in school.

"Yes. Except, nectar will kill any mortal that drinks it. Even demigods." She told me.

Good to know. I thought.

We kept walking for another few hours. I checked my working watch and saw it was around noon. Penelope had us break for lunch.

Rachael made a fire and started cooking soup that she made from ingredients from her bag. She handed me a bowl, and we started talking again. They explained more things about the school; like how there were different jobs each student had, and all the classes they had to take.

"We'll let Leo and Marchessa explain more, but there's battle and tactics classes, Greek history classes. Language classes. Most of them are taught by heads of dorms or Leo and Marchessa themselves." Penelope explained to me. She finally seemed to be warming up to me after finding out I was a werewolf, but she still looked at me with a mild degree of hate.

After everyone ate, we started moving again. I thought I would try to get along better with Penelope. Since we were traveling together and would be going to the same school, it didn't seem like a bad idea to be friends with the most powerful of Poseidon's children. Plus, she did smell amazing and was actually kind of pretty, but that's beside the point.

"So where is this school anyway, Penelope?" I asked her.

"Just outside Erie. We still have about a three-hour walk ahead of us."

I looked at my watch again, and it was going on after two. We must have been making good time since we left around seven in the morning. How we were going so far so quickly, I had no idea. Maybe some type of magic? Or was it just because we were demigods, we moved quicker? I decided not to question it.

"Hermes is decreasing our travel time. A one-time exception granted to us, thanks to Leo." Rachael explained, again, as if she was reading my mind.

"Hermes," I said, trying to remember what he was the god of.

Rachael filled in the blanks.

"God of travelers, messages, and thieves. Plus some other stuff."

I nodded. It was good to have a god in charge of traveling on your side when you're going hundreds of miles.

We kept walking without any further interruption. No monster attacks, no detours, straight to the school. There was one point when I picked up a distinct werewolf scent, but it wasn't normal. Something about it was older, more powerful. I didn't mention it to everyone else but did make it a point to try and move out of the way until the smell was gone.

Once we walked through a clearing, at about four o'clock in the afternoon, I noticed the same haze that was around Zeus' temple. As we got closer, the haze broke, revealing a massive white castle that seemed to shine in the mid-afternoon light.

"Jensen Smith, welcome to Ithaca, school of the gods," Rachael said with a huge smile on her face.

They lead me through a magnificent set of gates on the west side of the school. On either side of the doors were giant owls. Rachael looked at them with a delighted smile on her face. The walls around the school seemed to be three feet thick and made out of some sort of rock I wasn't able to identify, but it looked strong.

As my vanguard took me across the grounds, I looked around. Students were running everywhere, from what looked like forges that had smoke billowing from the chimneys, to what seemed to be an armory, based off of the sign that was written in Greek. Somehow I was able to read it.

Out in the distance, by a river that ran through the grounds by the east wall, there were students practicing sword fighting. Shields and swords clashed together, the sound rang out throughout the school ground.

My vanguard led me in through the large oak front doors of the school. The entrance hall looked amazing; made out of solid marble and gold. To my right was a door that, from what Rachael told me, lead to the mess hall. On my left, were two smaller doors. One labeled; Leo, the other; Marchessa. That was the direction that my new friends had taken me.

Rachael walked up to Leo's door, Blake up to Marchessa's, and they knocked at the same time. There was silence for a few seconds, and then the doors opened.

In front of me were two people that seemed to radiate power. Leo was a man that was about six inches taller than me, with short blonde hair. Marchessa was a little shorter than me, but with long black hair tied back in a ponytail. What shook me about them was their eyes. Leo's shone a bright navy blue, Marchessa's a deep blood red, like an alpha, but darker.

"Jensen, allow me to introduce you to Leonardo and Marchessa. Immortal headmasters of Ithaca." Rachael said.

Leo extended his hand to me.

"Nice to meet you, Jensen. How are you?"

I shook his hand.

"Not bad," I said.

"Well, that's good." Leo looked at Rachael and Rob.

"Robert Allan, please head to the infirmary and get that wound on your side checked, please. Sister, your shoulder seems to not be in any danger, but please have it looked at again by Megan after your debriefing."

"Yes, sir," Rob said, patting me on the back and walking toward the staircase at the back of the entrance hall.

"Brother, you don't seem to be injured. Come into my office." Marchessa said to Blake.

34

He nodded and entered.

"Glad you didn't get killed, Jensen." She added offhandedly as she turned around and closed the door.

"Don't mind her Jensen, she always a bit rude," Leo said.

"No worries," I told him because it didn't bother me.

"Please, you all, come in." Leo moved back, allowing Rachael, Penelope, Megan and I to enter.

Leo walked around us after closing the door and took a place behind a mahogany desk. I looked around the room and noticed that instead of walls, there were bookshelves. A few books were by great scientists like Aristotle and Newton. Others were war books like; The Art of War.

In front of Leo's desk were four chairs.

"Please take a seat." Leo motioned to the chairs, and we did.

"So, Jensen, I assume you have questions," Leo said.

"They were already answered," I told him, and it was true. My new friends explained everything I had already wanted to know.

Leo raised an eyebrow.

"Hmm, alright. Well, if you happen to think of anything, I implore you to ask."

I nodded, and then something popped into my mind.

"Sir, I do have one."

"Yes?"

"Why was I attacked in the first place?" I can't believe I hadn't asked this yet.

"Well, Jensen, that is a question I can only guess at." Leo started. "You do remember, I assume, that your father was the god that created werewolves, correct?"

I nodded.

"Yes, I assumed you would, being you're a direct descendant of Lycaon. Well, after Zeus created the werewolves, Lycaon increased his numbers vastly. He went from just over fifty werewolves to over a thousand in just under a year. After his numbers had grown, he waged war on Olympus."

I hadn't known that. Leo continued.

"After this war, which the gods had won, but barely, Zeus made a decree that no god shall every court a werewolf. You see, the werewolves were too powerful, and if one received the powers of a god, as most demigods do, the results could be catastrophic."

That didn't make sense.

"But, Zeus is my dad." I pointed out.

"Yes, and therein lies the problem. Zeus broke his decree, and not every other god is happy about this."

"So what you're saying is that one of the gods tried to kill me, just because Zeus broke this decree?"

Leo nodded.

"Yes, I'm sad to say that is the most likely situation."

I didn't say anything, trying to take this in.

"Do you know which god it was?" I asked.

"Well, that should be easy enough to deduce. Which monsters were you attacked by?"

"A hellhound, and the gorgons," I answered.

Leo's jaw dropped.

"There can only be one god that would be able to send both of those monsters after you. That god is Hades."

Hades, the god of the Underworld and treasures. He tried to kill me twice in twenty-four hours.

"When Hades wants you dead, Jensen, it is very hard to avoid it," Leo explained to me. "However, you managed to do it twice in one day."

Another question popped into my head.

"How did you know I was a werewolf, but my vanguard didn't?" I asked, trying to change the subject.

"I have been in contact with your mother ever since you were born. She always knew, someday, that you would come here. I didn't feel it necessary to inform your vanguard of this. It did not pertain to the mission at hand."

Again, I nodded.

"Now, Jensen, onto more pressing matters, at least in my mind." Leo chuckled, after a few moments of silence.

"Okay?" I had no idea what he was talking about.

"Hermes dropped off a message from your father this morning." He explained. "It's quite helpful. I assume, my darling sister explained to you the different powers a child of Zeus can possess, correct?"

I nodded.

"Well, Zeus has informed us which powers he has bestowed to you. Which is very rare, most demigods have to find out their powers on their own."

"Oh." That was all I could muster.

"Zeus has bestowed you, all of the powers given to his children. Including the one that we have not seen in centuries; the ability to generate your own lightning."

My friends all turned and looked at me at this point, amazed looks on their faces. I didn't know what to say. What made me so special?

"He also," Leo continued. "Sent a package with Hermes." Leo pulled a small package from one of the drawers in his desk.

It was only about the size of a necklace box. Leonardo handed it to me and I took it, hands trembling. Whether it was from rage or shock, I wasn't quite sure yet. I opened the package and revealed the contents inside.

The only thing in the box was a small, bronze flashlight. I picked it up and examined it.

"There were instructions," Leo said. "Zeus had Hephaestus design it to be practical to carry, but also deadly. If you channel electricity forward, towards the bulb, it will turn into a razor-sharp sword. Electricity channeled backward, towards the button, will transform it into a spear. A general zap will turn it into a shield."

"Does it work like a flashlight as well?" I asked since that was the only thing on my mind.

"I believe it does, by just clicking the button," Leo explained, laughing slightly.

I pressed the button, and sure enough, the light turned on.

At this point, I was starting to get angry, but I put the flashlight into my pocket without another word. My father was the god of all gods and didn't bother to be in my life until now. For some reason, now he wanted to give me a present, a weapon. Now, he decided to be there for me, without actually being there for me? Where did he get off? Before I could express any of this to the room, Leo interrupted.

"I understand feeling angry. When your parent is a god, it's hard not to feel abandoned. We have all felt that way. Trust me, it's for the best that they were not around. The gods, although powerful, cannot be everywhere at once."

I guess that made sense, but it didn't make me any less angry.

"As far as your training goes," Leo continued, "I will be the one teaching you how to use your powers. You will also attend language, tactics, and battle classes, as do all the students here."

I nodded.

"That's all I have for you now," Leo said. "Sister, if you and Penelope could stay behind, I would like to debrief both of you. Megan, if you could join Robert in the infirmary, make sure he's being taken care of. Also, if you could show Jensen to his dorm, I would greatly appreciate it."

My friends agreed, and Megan and I got up and left Leo's office. All I knew now, is that it was the weirdest first day of school I've ever had.

6

Chapter Six: My new room

Megan lead me up the large marble staircase at the back of the entrance hall. We climbed what seemed like, a hundred sets of stairs, but Megan mentioned that there were only forty. Still, by the time we got to the top floor, Megan was breathing deep.

"Here we are." She said. "Zeus dorm. Head on in, I have to get to the infirmary."

Megan ran back down the steps, as I stood alone in front of an oak door, with a golden lightning bolt engraved into the face. I gripped the bronze door handle and entered my dorm.

In front of me was what looked like a family living room, but way more extravagant. There was a television in the corner, that was currently off, two couches were against either wall. In the center of the room was a coffee table that was covered with magazines and board games; I noticed RISK in the mix. At the back of the room was a stone staircase that leads upstairs.

I walked toward it and headed upstairs. Now and then there was a landing with a door on either side. However, I didn't open any doors until I got to the very top, after about five staircases. There was a door in front me with a sign above it that read: Dorm head. That was me, so I opened the door.

Inside was a semi-large room, about twelve feet by twelve feet. In the middle was a four-post bed made out of iron with curtains hanging around it. On the far left wall, a window overlooked the grounds. I walked over to it and stared straight out.

The view was magnificent. I figured I was in the tallest tower since from what I could tell, there were no more stairs in the entire castle. Taking my bag off and setting it on the floor, I sat down on the bed. I took the flashlight from my pocket and examined it again. Rage suddenly filled me as it had downstairs in Leo's office.

My father didn't even bother to be a part of my life. I set the flashlight down on the nightstand beside my bed. Looking around the room, I saw in the corner next to the door was a dresser, and what seemed to be a mannequin for armor.

I stood up and began to put my clothes in the dresser. When I was done, I looked inside my bag and remembered the money my Uncle Jack had given me. I took it out of its pocket and slipped it inside a pair of socks for safekeeping.

After I had sat back down, I heard a knocking on the door downstairs. I made my way down slowly. When I opened the door Rachael's happy, smiling face was staring back at me. Her eyes gleaming.

"Leo wanted me to ask you if you would like your first lesson today before dinner." She said.

I looked at my watch and realized it was only six o'clock.

"Sure," I said I figured the quicker I learned how to use my powers the better.

I followed Rachael onto the landing, closing the door behind me. Rachael started talking the second we began walking.

"How do you like your room?" She asked.

"It's nice. A really good view out of my window."

"I've never been in there before since there haven't been any children of Zeus here since I started."

"When did you get here?" I just remembered I never bothered to ask Rachael any questions about herself.

"Oh, when I was ten. My dad got tired of monster attacks. He asked my mother, in prayer, for somewhere safe for me. She led him here."

"Didn't he want you around?"

"Oh, yes he did. My father loves me, but me being there was just too dangerous. I go and see them almost every summer unless a quest needs to be done and I get picked for it."

"They send you out on quests? Isn't that dangerous?"

"Yes, but that's why we're here Jensen. We learn how to protect ourselves to not only live

in the normal world, but also to help the gods anyway we can."

At this point, we were about halfway down the staircase.

"So how did Leo and Marchessa become immortal?" I asked.

"They were hand-picked by Athena and Ares. They've been teachers here for over a

thousand years, but they didn't create the school. They were the best students when they attended and completed the most quests."

"Oh. That's pretty cool." I said.

"Yeah, it's not a bad deal they got." Rachael laughed.

I looked over the rail and saw we were only about fifty feet up from the ground floor.

"You want an express trip down?" I asked Rachael.

"What?"

Without waiting for her to answer, I put my arm around her waist. I felt her tighten up, and when I looked at her face, she was blushing. Trying to ignore this, I vaulted over the banister. With a thud, I hit the ground. When I let Rachael go, she just looked at me.

"You're awesome." She said quietly, and the cleared her throat. "Leo's in his office. I'm

going to do patrol duty with Blake, he said you can join us after dinner." She ran off, out the front doors.

That was awkward. I thought.

I walked to Leo's office door and knocked. A few seconds later, the blue-eyed headmaster answered.

"Ah, Jensen. I was hoping you would want to start today." He said cheerfully. "We'll be

training outside today. I would hate to blow my office up with a lightning bolt."

I followed Leo out the front doors and down the steps. He led me to a combat ring, that currently had people practicing with spears. Penelope was going hard against a guy around my age with short blonde hair and pointed nose. She seemed to be sweating a lot, and the kid she was fighting seemed to be moving like a blur, dodging every strike.

"We'll wait until they're done," Leo said. "It shouldn't belong."

He was right.

As if predicting his movements, Penelope stabbed, the kid dodged it, but Penelope kicked where he was going to move, and sent him flying backward. Leo clapped.

"Good job Penny. Andrew, please, if you don't mind, Jensen and I require the combat ring."

Andrew nodded, and walked off towards the school, followed by Penelope, who gave me a sideways glance. I couldn't tell if it was malicious, or kind.

Leo stepped into the middle of the ring, and I followed him, standing a few feet away from him.

"Okay, Jensen. The first thing I'm going to teach you is lightning summoning and control." Leo said.

I nodded but didn't quite know how he was going to do that.

"First, you need to concentrate. One thing to remember is the sky is at your control. You are the son of Zeus."

Leo pulled his sword from his side and handed it to me.

"It will be easier for you to direct the lightning through an object, normally a weapon. Once you get better, you can forgo the weapon and just summon lightning strikes on your own."

"So, what do I have to do," I asked.

"Concentrate on a lightning bolt, coming out of the air, striking your sword, and flowing in the direction you point it. I would prefer it if you did not point it at me." He said with a chuckle.

I nodded again and closed my eyes.

I did as Leo had instructed, and concentrated on lightning coming down from the sky, striking my sword, and flying towards the river, which is where I was pointing the sword. The problem was, the sword I was using felt weird in my hands; off-balance. I tried not to let it bother me.

After standing there for about a minute, something happened. The hairs on my arm and neck stood straight up. I heard a clap of thunder and opened my eyes. As I opened them, a lightning bolt came from the sky, hit my sword, and exploded on the river bank.

Leo clapped.

"You're a natural! It takes most students weeks to achieve that." He explained. "Now, try it a few more times, with your eyes open. If you are to use this in a battle, you obviously can't stand there with your eyes closed."

I did as he instructed. Each time I summoned lightning, I felt a little more drained, but it was getting easier. Soon, after about an hour, I was able to call a lightning strike instantly and direct it anyway I wanted to.

After I sent a lightning bolt flying over the wall and right past Rachael, who was

patrolling the perimeter, Leo called for me to stop. The sun was setting.

"Very good, Jensen! Very good." He said with a smile. "Tomorrow, we'll work on controlling wind currents. It's the same process of concentration. Given enough time, you should even be able to lift yourself off the ground. After you get that down, I'll teach you to create your own lightning, and you'll be able to use that new weapon you have."

"Awesome," I said.

"It's going on fifteen past eight, time for dinner."

I handed Leo back his sword and followed him inside. He led me into the dining hall.

The dining hall was huge. The ceiling went up about a hundred feet, torches all around the walls that gave a very bright light. There were tables all over the place, several dozens, I figured they were for all the different dorms. Rob waved at me from the Hephaestus table on the left side of the room. I waved back.

There was a big table at the back of the dining hall that had as many chairs as there were tables. Leo lead me there.

"Being the head of Zeus dorm, you always have a seat at the head table. Right next to me." He said as we sat down, him in the middle next to Marchessa, who was already seated, me in the chair to his right.

Rob came running up to the head table a few moments later and took his spot three chairs down from me.

"How was training?" He asked. "I heard the thunder from the infirmary."

"Good. Satisfying." I told him because it was.

A few moments later Megan and Penelope entered the dining hall and took their seats at the table; Megan to Rob's right, and Penelope right next to me. After another few minutes, the entire dining hall was filled with demigods, and all the seats at the head table were taken, besides Rachael's and Blakes, who were still on patrol.

Leo stood.

"Ladies and Gentlemen," he said, and the chatter in the room died. "First, before dinner, we have a few announcements. I would like to formally introduce you all to our newest student, Jensen Smith, son of Zeus!"

There was slight applause while everyone in the room looked at me. I waved.

"Secondly, please make sure that you are all doing your part in maintaining and protecting this school. There have been several missed patrols over the last few days. For the rest, I give the floor to Marchessa." He said as he took his seat.

Marchessa stood now.

"The final announcement pertains to the one Leonardo just shared. If there is one more missed patrol, you will answer to me." She said forcefully. "We must do everything we can to protect this school and our students." She sat down, ending her speech.

I had no idea what she meant by answering to her, but I know I didn't want to find out. Leo stood up again.

"Now, with that bit of unpleasantness behind us, please enjoy your meal."

From behind us, men were exiting doors that I hadn't noticed before. These men, with furry legs and hooves, were carrying trays of every kind of food you could ever want; pizza, burgers, lamb, mashed potatoes, fries. I was in heaven. I took a little bit of everything, not noticing until then how hungry I was.

Reaching over to a pitcher, I poured myself some water. I looked over at Penelope, and she was giving me a really weird look.

"What's up?" I asked.

"Nothing." She said, now looking anywhere but at me.

"Listen," I said. "I don't understand why you don't like me, but I'd like to change that if at all possible."

She looked back at me.

"I don't have a problem with you. I have a problem with your father."

"Oh." I didn't know what to say. "Is it the rivalry?" I asked.

"No. You wouldn't get it." She told me.

"Try me," I said. "You'd be surprised."

She took a deep breath.

"I don't even know why I'm going to tell you this."

"Because you know I'm a nice guy? And if I wanted to, I could probably give you a really good set of puppy dog eyes." I suggested with a smile.

She chuckled, which was a good sign. Penelope took a bite of her lamb before continuing.

"Zeus killed my first boyfriend, about two years ago."

"Your boyfriend that was a werewolf?" I asked.

She nodded, a tear now in her eyes.

"Um, I'm sorry." I offered.

"It's not your fault, Jensen. Zeus has always hated werewolves, that's the only reason he killed him. He was traveling to Nevada to visit family, and Zeus blew his plane out of the sky. He was the only one that died."

"If Zeus has always hated werewolves, why do I exist?" I asked.

She shook her head.

"Absolutely no idea." She told me, looking at me again. "That's kind of why I haven't talked to you or anything since we got back. I'm so mad at Zeus."

Thunder echoed outside. It gave me a weird chill down my spine. I took a few bites of my pizza before I said anything else.

"Well, if it helps at all, if I ever meet my father, I'll make sure that I put an end to the needless werewolf killings. I'll also try my best to get you an apology." I told her. I don't know why I was offering this to her because I barely knew her. However, I felt like Penelope and I had a connection, and a strong one.

"Thanks, Jensen." She said, a smile now on her face.

"No problem, Penelope."

"It's Penny." She told me.

"So we're friends now?" I asked with a smirk.

"Shut up and eat." She ordered and turned back to her plate.

Once we had finished eating, and I was honestly sad it was over because that was the best meal I've ever had, I walked out of the dining hall and out the front doors. The sky had become darker since I came inside. Rachael saw me immediately and waved me over. I ran over to the east wall and jumped up the twenty feet high wall to join her and Blake.

They both were decked out in bronze plated armor with bow and quiver on their backs, shield, and sword in hand.

"What's up, Jensen?" Blake asked.

"Rachael said I should join you guys on patrol after dinner," I explained.

He nodded. Rachael blushed.

"Let's go get you some weapons," Rachael said and started walking toward a ladder little ways down the wall.

"Come here," I told her, and put my arm around her as I had on the stairs. With Rachael at my side, I jumped down from the wall and landed softly on the grass. I let her go, she was still blushing. She led me over to the armory.

When she opened the door, I saw a vast array of weapons and armor; bows, swords, spears, shields. Rachael moved back, letting me have full access to everything inside. After looking over everything for a minute or so, I picked a simple bronze sword and iron chest plate.

"That's it?" She asked.

"I shouldn't need much. I heal quick." I laughed. "Let's go."

We started walking back over to the wall.

"So what are we patrolling for?" I asked her.

"Monsters. If any get too close, we have to take them out." She explained.

I nodded, and a question popped into my head.

"Why do the monsters burst into flame when they die?" I asked, remembering my encounter with the gorgons.

"They burn back to the Underworld and Tartarus. Monsters very rarely die for good. Hades normally selects which monsters come back. He'll bring back smaller monsters that regenerate quickly, like hellhounds, mormo, and dracaena. More powerful monsters; the gorgons, the manticore, giants, they normally break out on their own. They take a while to reform normally though."

"That's, creepy," I told her. She laughed.

We had reached the wall and Rachael started climbing the ladder while I jumped up as I had before.

Rachael, Blake and I patrolled the walls for a few more hours. We talked, just generally getting to know each other better. Blake told me how his mom lived in Florida, and he would visit her every summer and holidays. Rachael told me that she was sad she missed dinner because they served pizza today; her favorite food.

There were no monster attacks, that was, until about midnight.

We were doing our final walk around the wall. When we were almost at the ladder, there was a loud howl from the distance.

"Hellhound," I told the others.

"What?" They said at the same time. Apparently, it was farther away than I thought.

"There's a hellhound," I listened a little more closely. "About a mile away to the east."

"You're really awesome," Rachael said under her breath. This time I blushed.

Before I could say anything else, however, there was another howl, this time from the west. This one was much closer, so close, that even Blake and Rachael heard it, and a few lights in the castle had turned on and started flooding the grounds with light from the windows.

I heard trees crashing, coming from both directions of the howls. Before I knew what was happening, there were five hellhounds, about a hundred yards away from the gates of the school.

Rachael sheathed her sword and swapped her shield for her bow and arrow.

Blake slid down the ladder and ran out the front gates.

Is he crazy? I thought. He's seriously going to take on five hellhounds at once?

I wasn't about to let that happen.

I jumped down behind him while Rachael let a few arrows fly. Running quickly, I caught up with Blake. He was raising his shield, ready for a fight.

"Hang on!" I told him and grabbed his arm. "I've got an idea."

I raised my sword and concentrated. The hellhounds were only a few feet away now, getting ready to pounce. I pushed Blake to the side and summoned a lightning bolt from the sky. It came down, ricocheted off my blade, and caught two of the hellhounds. Quickly, I rolled out of the way to avoid the other three.

Blake came running at one of them and jumped through the flames of the two hellhounds that were burning. He jammed his blade right in between the hellhounds shoulder blades as it crouched after hitting the ground. It let out a whine of pain and started to burn away.

I threw my blade like a throwing knife at another, sadly, it missed by about ten feet. However, I didn't have to worry about it because an arrow came from the wall and caught the monster directly between the eyes, just as it turned to me, fangs bared. I looked back at Rachael, who had a big smile on her face.

The final hellhound wasn't deterred, however. It took a swipe at Blake with its paw and caught him right in the chest. He went flying, about thirty feet and hit the ground hard, unmoving. The monster tried the same thing with me, but I jumped over its attack and shifted. When I landed, I looked the hellhound directly in the eyes, my sky blue glow reflecting off of its deep black.

It tried to bite me, but I dodged that as well. I slid underneath the stomach of the monster and stopped directly below it. Quickly and powerfully, I jabbed my claws deep into its midsection. The hellhound stopped moving and started to burst into flames, beginning at my hand. After it had dissolved completely, I turned back to Blake.

I ran back over to him as quickly as I could.

"Blake, are you okay?" I asked as I crouched next to him

I tuned my hearing and caught the sound of his heartbeat. Good, he was alive, just knocked out. Rachael came up behind me, sweat on her face.

"Lots of people came out to see what was going on." She told me. "Is he okay?"

I nodded.

"Just knocked out. I'm gonna get him inside." I said and picked up Blake.

Carrying him carefully, I took him past the gates and met a crowd of about fifty people. Everyone was looking at me, and at that point, I remembered I hadn't returned to normal. I shifted back to my normal form.

Ignoring everyone as best as I could, I took Blake inside and then realized I had no idea where the infirmary is. Megan saved me from having to figure it out.

She came running in from outside, her medical bag in her hands.

"Come on." She said, running up the stairs. I followed.

She took me to the third floor, down a long hallway, and into a big room that was filled with medical beds. I looked around but didn't see any modern medical equipment, just some cabinets with golden and bronze instruments and jars filled with herbs and liquids.

"Set him here," Megan said, motioning to the first bed on the left.

I set him down, and Megan got to work doing, whatever it was you could do for someone who was knocked unconscious. Before I knew it, Blake had woken up.

"Thanks, Jensen." He said weakly.

"No problem, man."

"He needs rest," Megan said. "Thanks for bringing him in, we're good. You should go to bed, it's late, I'll look after him."

"Feel better, Blake," I said and walked out of the infirmary.

I walked back down the hallway, opened the door to the staircase and was greeted by Rachael and Leo.

"He's fine," I told them. "Megan's looking after him."

"Very good," Leo said. "I shall check on him anyway, just to be sure. Good work, Jensen. Not bad for a first patrol."

He smiled and walked past me toward the infirmary. Rachael just looked at me.

"Let me guess," I laughed. "I'm awesome?"

She smiled and blushed again.

"Yeah."

"I'm going to bed," I told her. "See you in the morning?"

"Definitely." She said and walked back downstairs.

When I got back to my dorm, I went straight upstairs to my room, took my armor off and set it on the stand next to my dresser. I still felt really energized, like electricity was pumping through my body, and I got a really weird idea.

I picked my flashlight up from my bedside table and started to concentrate. Imagining a small shock of lightning coming from my hand, I willed it to travel towards the bulb. After a few minutes and a lot of tries, there was a very small pop and the smell of ozone, like chlorine, or the smell before a storm. When I looked down, instead of holding a flashlight, I was holding a bronze razor-sharp sword, about two feet in length.

Awesome. I thought. One last thing I have to learn.

I willed the lightning from my body again and changed the sword into a shield with a sharp zap in the center of the hilt of the sword. It was bronze as well and had lightning bolts and clouds engraved into the face.

Again, I willed more lightning into the grip on the shield, this time towards the back, and instead of a shield, I held a spear that was five feet long, with a bronze tip. At least I had mastered this as well. I sent another shock of lightning towards the back again, and my spear turned back into a flashlight.

The sensation of lightning traveling through my body was very weird. It wasn't like anything else I had ever felt. Almost like a shiver that would go away after a few moments.

I set the flashlight back down on my nightstand and lay back into my bed, pulling the curtains closed. It was a lot to take in for one day, but it was easily the coolest first day of school I've ever had.

7

Chapter Seven: First day of class

I was woken up the next morning by a pounding on the downstairs door. When I checked my watch, I saw it was only six in the morning. Despite this, I felt completely rested. I quickly put on some clothes, grabbed the watch/shield Rob had made me, and my flashlight, and ran to open the door. Rob was standing there waiting for me.

"Breakfast time, man. Then class. You're following my schedule for now."

"Got it," I said and followed him down the stairs.

He started telling me how his motorbike was coming. Apparently, he had installed a brand new location and retrieval system. He showed me his own watch, and it looked a lot like mine, just a bronze watch with a regular face. His, however, had several more buttons around the edge, Rob pointed to one near the bottom.

"If I press that, in theory, the bike will come to me within a hundred-mile range." He explained.

"That's pretty impressive," I said because it was.

We reached the bottom of the staircase and started walking toward the dining hall. As we made our way up to the head table, kids all around the room started looking at me and whispering.

"Um, you know why they're doing that?" I whispered to Rob.

"They all saw you in full wolf mode last night. The ones that didn't, were told. Word travels like wildfire around here. My siblings were up all night

51

talking about it. Most haven't ever seen a werewolf."

"Cool," I said, sarcastically.

When we reached the head table and took our seats, I noticed that Rachael and Blake were both here. Blake seemed to have a few bruises but otherwise looked okay.

"How are you feeling?" I asked, pouring myself some water from the pitcher.

"Alive. A little sore." He answered.

"Good to know," I said with a smile.

A few moments later, Penelope walked in followed by Leonardo and Marchessa. They all took their places, Leo and Penelope on either side of me. Once they were all settled and the other heads of the dorms sat down, the goat men brought out trays of breakfast food; eggs, bacon, pancakes, waffles. They also had toppings; blueberries, chocolate, strawberries. I took some waffles, bacon, chocolate, and strawberries and loaded my plate. Then I remembered a question I had last night but was too hungry to bother to ask.

"Those are saytrs, right?" I asked, leaning towards Penny.

She nodded, her mouth full of eggs. She swallowed.

"Yeah. They were placed here for regular duties by Dionysus. God of wine. Better them be here than out in the world. Less messy that way. They're nice enough though." She explained.

It felt good being on speaking terms with Penny, friends actually. She was really nice after she stopped hating your guts, plus, she always smelled like strawberries. That's beside the point.

I leaned over towards Leo now, trying to make sure he could hear me over the conversation in the room.

"There's one less thing you need to teach me."

He looked at me, curiously.

"Is that so?" He said with a smile.

I pulled my flashlight out from my pocket, focused a small jolt of electricity towards the front, and held my sword in my hand. This one actually felt balanced.

"Very nice. Now just to turn that lightning you're using for that into a bolt and were good to go." He said, looking impressed.

I changed my sword back into a flashlight and put it back in my pocket.

"We'll have another lesson then after your classes. Since you're following Robert's schedule, you can meet me in the combat ring around three, I already have it reserved." Leo explained to me.

I nodded and turned back to my breakfast.

Once I was done eating, Rob came up and clapped me on the back.

"The first class starts in ten minutes. Language. Greek." He told me. "Come on."

I got up and followed Rob out of the dining hall.

"Where's the class?" I asked him.

"Third floor. First door on the left."

"Who teaches it?"

He looked at me and flashed me a smirk.

"Rachael." He laughed.

Why that was funny, I had no idea, so I just followed him up to the third floor and into the classroom.

The room wasn't too impressive. It looked like a normal classroom you would see in any school, but there were weapons and armor all over the walls. Rob and I sat in the back right next to each other. A few moments later, Rachael walked in.

She saw Rob and I sitting in the back, and I could see her face blush. She cleared her throat.

"It's funny to see you here early, Rob." She said.

"I figured I would give Jensen a good first impression. Don't get used to it." He called back.

Rachael laughed and started to pull books out of her backpack and placing them on the table.

"So how do classes work since the dorm heads teach?"

"Well, some of us take classes all day. Mostly about our own subject. Like my siblings all take my class in the forges. That's not until the afternoon though. We all have to take basic classes though, like language, battle training, and tactics."

"Let me guess, Rachael teaches language and tactics. Blake teaches battle training."

He nodded.

"Though, today, since Blake's all banged up from last night, we'll probably get Marchessa." He laughed.

"She bad?" I asked.

"Just make sure you catch on quick. She doesn't let up, even if you're new."

The conversation ended there due to the classroom filling up with other students. I noticed some people with the same eyes as Penny, who sat upfront. Once everyone was seated, Rachael started the class.

I've got to say, even though I'm not a big foreign language guy, Rachael made it interesting. She went over literally every part of the Greek language. I like to think of myself as a fast learner, so by the end of the two-hour class, I was more or less fluent. Rob slept the entire time.

"Why do you even show up if you fall asleep?" I asked as we were leaving, heading down to the grounds for battle training.

"I already know it all, but Leo won't let me stop going until I pass the final at the end of the year."

"If you know it all, why haven't you passed?" I was confused.

"Well, first two times I slept through it and only got my name down. Last time I was on a quest, wasn't here for it. He didn't give me an excuse though."

I pondered this for a moment as we walked down the front steps of the school and headed over to the same combat ring that Leo and I used last night.

Sure enough, Marchessa was standing there, sword and shield out, waiting for us. Blake was out there too, but sitting in a chair off to the side. Once the entire class gathered around, about twenty of us, Marchessa started.

"Well, we have a new one today." She said, pointing the tip of her sword at me. "You'll be with me. Break up into pairs, and start sparing."

Rob gave me a good luck look and paired up with one of his younger siblings.

I walked up to Marchessa, and pulled my flashlight out of my pocket and turning it into a sword.

"Got a shield?" She asked, and I pressed the button on my watch.

Instantly, my bronze shield popped out.

"Good, you'll need it."

She started off by showing me basic thrusting, slashing, and parrying. Again, I'm a pretty quick learner, so soon I was going toe to toe with Marchessa. She was right, I did need my shield, but I was fighting like I had been doing it my entire life, she even said so. At one point, I was doing so good, the entire class had stopped and looked. Blake was on the edge of his seat.

Marchessa slashed at me, and I blocked it with my shield, at the same time, I turned my sword into a spear. She dodged my stab easily, and I transformed it back into a sword as Marchessa stabbed into my leg. I wasn't quick enough and the blade went straight through and stuck into the ground. Taking my opportunity in between the stabs of pain, I used some of my strength and kicked the blade with my good leg, snapping it in half.

Using my shield, I knocked Marchessa's out of her hand. She moved back a few paces, defenseless. I raised my blade to her neck, blood still dripping out of my healing leg. She looked at me and snapped her fingers. My sword point immediately fell to the ground, like I was unable to lift it. Considering how I could lift more than three tons easily, this was weird.

"I can't use that move often, and I hardly ever have to, but good job Jensen," Marchessa said. "You still have some work to do, but not bad."

I looked around at the rest of the class, who was still looking at me. Rob caught my eyes and started a slow clap, silently laughing. No one joined in, they were all standing there in shocked silence.

"Blake, you notice any problems throughout the class?" Marchessa turned and asked.

"No, ma'am. Everyone looked pretty good." Blake answered.

"Class dismissed."

Rob ran up to me and clapped me on the back as I was pulling Marchessa's, now broken sword from my leg. Changing my weapons back to normal, I checked my real watch, and it was already eleven. How did three hours go by so fast?

"Dude, nobody, not even Blake, has taken down Marchessa like that." He explained.

I didn't know what to say, so I didn't say anything.

"You want Megan to look at your leg?" He asked, kind of concerned.

"Nah, It's all good. It already healed." I said, pulling my jean leg up to show him.

"That's seriously the most impressive thing I've seen in my life." He looked at my leg longingly.

"Don't ask," I told him.

"Don't ask what?" He said, looking me in my eyes now.

"Don't ask me to turn you. One, I can't, I'm not an alpha or delta. Two, it's not all it's cracked up to be."

"But, I mean, you know someone who could turn me. Plus, aren't all the cool powers worth it?" He smiled.

"Not all the time. Anywhere I go, if there aren't any other werewolves, it's like I'm an outcast. You see how everyone besides you guys look at me. They think I'm a freak."

We walked into the entrance hall and stopped outside the dining hall doors.

"They don't think that. Trust me, man. I get your point, and I won't ask, but they don't think you're a freak. They've just either never seen one, or haven't seen a werewolf in a long time."

I pushed open the doors to the dining hall and started walking to the head table.

"Yeah, maybe you're right."

I sat down next to Penny at the head table.

"What's wrong?" She asked.

I shook my head.

"Nothing, just a talk Rob and I had. I'm good." I told her and smiled.

Now that we were talking, she had a way of making me smile out of nowhere, even though we hadn't known each other long. Maybe it was her smell of strawberries.

Lunch started, but I was still kind of full from breakfast, so I just grabbed a ham sandwich from one of the saytrs.

"Do you want to spar a little after your training with Leo tonight? Maybe after dinner?" Penny asked me.

I looked at her for a few seconds before answering.

"Su… sure." I stammered. "After dinner." I was genuinely surprised she asked me to do something.

I hadn't noticed Rachael was standing behind us, getting ready to talk to one of us, but after I agreed to spar with Penny, Rachael went to her seat and sat down. She looked mad. I thought it best not to ask her about it.

After we ate lunch, Rob and I had battle tactics on the fourth floor, with Rachael teaching. That class lasted about three hours. Rachael went over a phalanx and different flanking patterns. It was actually really useful information, and I made sure I paid close attention. However, it was hard when every five minutes, Rachael was giving me weird looks.

Once the class let out, I checked my watch. It was still only a quarter to three, so I decided to hang back for a bit.

"Everything okay?" I asked Rachael after telling Rob I would see him at dinner and the room had emptied.

She looked up at me from her desk, just realizing I was the only one there.

"I'm okay." She said stiffly.

"You just seemed a little upset at lunch, and kind of all through the class," I said awkwardly.

"Oh, well I heard you and Penny talking. I was just going to ask if you wanted to patrol tonight, but it's okay. Megan's doing it with me instead."

"Oh, okay. So we're alright?"

She nodded.

"I'll see you at dinner, Jensen." She said, gathering up her papers and leaving the room.

I will never understand girls. I thought as I walked downstairs to my lesson with Leo.

When I arrived at the combat ring, Leo was already standing there, sword in hand.

"Jensen! Welcome! I believe today, I promised we would work on wind control?" He

said.

"Yes, sir," I responded.

"Well, you remember what we did with the lightning? Do that, but with a wind current.

Imagine the wind is surging around you, lifting you up. If that proves to be too much, we can try with a smaller object." Leo explained.

I nodded and started to concentrate, just as Leo instructed. It took me a few minutes, but I was getting it. My feet started to lift up off of the ground. I felt like there was a platform under my feet, but there was no ground to be seen.

I was rising higher and higher, and soon, I was at least twenty feet off the ground. As I

lowered myself to the ground, Leo was standing there clapping.

"You're a very fast learner, Jensen. No one has ever gotten these abilities faster than you." He was saying as I touched down.

"I try my best," I told him.

"Well, since that didn't even take you half an hour to master, why don't we move on to controlling your inner lightning?" He recommended.

Before he could say any more, I got the picture. All of these abilities were all about control, and concentration. Without any further instruction, I concentrated all of the electricity I could and raised my arm. A few seconds later, a bolt of lightning shot out of my fingertips, exploding in the river where I was aiming.

When I looked back at Leo, his mouth was open.

"Good job. I honestly don't think there's anything else to teach you in regards to this. All it is now is coming up with your own ways to use these abilities. I feel like you'll find a good use for them." He said and sheathed his sword.

"Thanks. I'll see what I can do. I know I'm not going to be using the stairs for a while." I laughed.

Leo and I walked inside, and he went into his office. I decided I'd try to talk to Rachael again. When I sniffed the air, I immediately caught her scent. A distinct orange shampoo that I hadn't smelled anywhere else.

Using the wind, I lifted myself to the eighth floor and knocked on the door. I stared at the bronze owl that was secured to the door for a few moments before the door opened. One of Rachael's little sisters, about ten years old, was standing there.

"Um, is Rachael in there?" I asked.

She nodded and ran back inside. A few moments later, Rachael came onto the landing, closing the door behind her.

"Yes?" She said, not looking at me.

"I wanted to say I'm sorry. I didn't know you wanted me to do patrol tonight with you." I explained awkwardly.

She took a deep breathe then looked in my eyes.

"It's fine. I overreacted. I just thought, maybe, we could talk some more, get to know each other better."

I perked up a little.

"I'd like that. I really would. What do you say tomorrow, I'll do patrol with you. If you're scheduled I mean?"

"I make the schedule, so yeah, we can do that." She laughed.

"Well good. I'm going to head down to the forges, see what Robs doing. I'll see you at dinner?"

She nodded with a smile and walked back into her dorm, a skip in her step.

I jumped over the banister and let the air cushion my fall. I really was getting the hang of this pretty quickly. After I landed I walked out the front doors and headed to the forges. Rob was outside, working on his motorcycle.

"How's it going?" I asked him as he slid out from under the bike.

"Good, just recalibrating the greek fire emitter." He explained, wiping oil off of his shirt.

"Nice. Is the bike almost done?"

"Couple more adjustments, then I think so." He said with a smile.

I nodded.

"I'm glad you came down actually. I need your help with a project."

"Sure. What is it?"

He pointed up on the walls at all of the giant crossbows.

"They need to be calibrated and modified. Normally, we use a crane we made to take them down since they're about two tons each, but I figured since you were here, you'd be able to do it? Save us some time?"

I nodded again.

"Yeah, shouldn't be a problem. You want to get started on that now?" I asked.

"Let's go." He said as he got up.

Today was particularly hot, about ninety degrees. Rob and I took our shirts off and started to work. I jumped up the east wall, carrying Rob with me. He loosened the bolts on the mount for the first crossbow, and I let it fall into my hands. It was pretty heavy, like Rob said, about two tons, but it wasn't even anywhere close to my max. I jumped down off the wall and took the crossbow to the forge entrance so Rob's siblings could start on the modifications.

It took them about twenty minutes to do them, so they were done by the time I had come back with the second one from the south wall. I picked up the completed crossbow and yelled at Rob to meet me at the first mount. When I jumped up the wall and slid the crossbow in its mount, Rob quickly secured and calibrated it.

As we worked, some of the other students gathered around, watching me.

"You know what that's about?" I asked Rob as we were securing the second crossbow.

"Probably, because they've never seen anybody lift something like that without breaking a sweat." He guessed. "Let's keep working. Just ignore them."

We repeated the process around the entire wall on all four crossbows. Once we were done, I checked my watch. It was about a quarter past six, dinner had already started. Rob and I grabbed our shirts and walked into the school, and took our spots at the head table. Everyone was already there, and food had already been served. Saytrs were still walking around with trays, however, so I grabbed a large pile of roast beef and mashed potatoes.

"So, you ready to spar after dinner?" Penny asked me.

I swallowed my food, nodding my head.

"Most definitely."

We finished eating after about half an hour and excused ourselves from the head table. Penny and I walked out of the front doors. I walked to the combat ring, while Penny went to the armory to retrieve her weapons and armor.

When she returned, I already had my flashlight out of my pocket, waiting for Penny to start.

"Ready?" She asked with a smirk.

I nodded, changing my flashlight into a sword.

Penny charged me all out, shield raised. She swiped at me with her sword, and I easily parried her attack. She kept pressing harder. This went on for a few minutes, she really seemed like she was trying to kill me, but all the while she had a smile on her face.

I thought I should try to feign her, let her think she was getting under my guard, but I messed up. Her sword expertly passed under my block and sank into my leg. Penny had a look of shock on her face. I used a wind current to knock her back, admittedly it was a little too strong. She flew back and landed in the river about fifty feet away.

I pulled her sword out of my leg and threw it by the point into the ground. My wound healed almost instantly. I ran over to the river to see if Penny was okay. When I got there, a huge, swirling tower of water, at least thirty feet high, erupted from the river. Penny was standing in the middle of it.

She walked out of the river, the tower of water still spinning around her, following her as she went.

"We're still going?" I asked her.

She nodded and raised her arms.

The tower of water surged towards me. I wasn't quick enough and was picked up by the water. It pushed me around, entered my lungs, almost drowning me until I was pushed out of the top like a rocket. I flew at least fifty feet higher in the air. As I was spiraling out of control, I tried my best to use the wind currents to steady me. It worked, and then I channeled a wind current to send me to the ground.

When I landed, Penny was back in the combat ring, her sword, and shield in her hands. I raised my own sword and channeled my internal lightning through it. It hit Penny's shield and sent her flying backward. She hit the ground hard, her weapons falling out of her hands.

I ran over to her and knelt at her side. She raised her head.

"You okay?" I asked.

"Yeah. I think you win." She said with a smile, a bruise forming on her cheek.

I extended a hand and helped her up. She collected her weapons and returned them to the armory.

"Do you want to go somewhere to study?" She asked me.

"Sure. Battle tactics?" I suggested.

She nodded and we headed inside and up the stairs to my dorm after grabbing Penny's books. When we got inside, Penny sat on one of the couch and opened her books and notes on the coffee table. I sat down next to her and we started going over the different battle tactics.

We were going over flanking and phalanx maneuvers. Every now and then I would catch Penny looking at me, but whenever I did, she quickly went back to her books.

After a while, I decided that we had gone over everything that I could process. For it only being my second day, there was a lot of information. I checked my watch. It was just after midnight.

"You know if Leo or Marchessa catch you up here this late, we'll be in a lot of trouble, right?"

"Yeah." She said, checking her own watch. "I better go."

She packed her books and notes back into her bag and walked to the door.

"See you tomorrow?" She asked.

"Sure thing," I said.

Penny smiled and left.

I went up to bed, thinking about the looks she was giving me while we studied. Her strawberry smell still lingered in the dorm. I went to bed in a really good mood.

8

Chapter Eight: An extended outing

The next few weeks seemed to fly by. I spent my days in class and mastering my new powers. Most nights I would spend with Rachael and Blake, once he was healthy, on patrol. Normally after dinner, Penny and I would study, sometimes accompanied by Megan. Rob and I would work on things around the school; traps, weapons, and vehicles mostly.

One day, after I had been at the school for about a month and a half, Rachael and I were on patrol, it was around midnight. We were walking across the south wall. The moon was full and cast a bright light from the cloudless sky. In the distance, I heard a few werewolves howling. Rachael stopped in the middle of the wall, looking at me.

"What's up?" I asked, stopping a few feet in front of her.

"Can I ask you a question, Jensen?" She asked.

"Sure." I chuckled.

We had gotten to know each other pretty well lately, and I really didn't think she needed permission to ask me a question.

"What do you think of me?"

I thought that was a weird question.

"Why?"

"I'm just wondering." She said, blushing.

"Well, I think you're super nice and funny and you are a lot of fun to be around. You're a good friend."

"Oh." She said, blushing a deeper shade of red. "What do you think of Penny?"

The truth is, I didn't know. I really liked Penny. She always made me laugh, no matter what, and I really liked spending time with her. Way more than any of my other friends. I explained most of that to Rachael, taking out the part of liking to spend time with Penny more, that seemed kind of insensitive.

"Oh," Rachael said again.

"Everything okay?" I asked her.

"Well, I was just wondering, if maybe, before summer break started, if you wanted to maybe head into town with me, and get dinner or something." She said, not looking at me.

I thought that was a weird way to ask me to hang out.

"Sure. That would be a lot of fun." I told her.

Her eyes snapped back to me, a smile now on her face.

"How about tomorrow?" She asked.

"Sounds good to me. Let's finish this patrol." I said and started walking again.

We walked the wall together for another two hours until the shift change. I flew Rachael up to her floor and dropped her off at her door. After I dropped her off, I flew to my own dorm and walked inside, climbed the stairs, and went to bed. Sadly, that was the last good night's sleep I would get for a while.

I woke up the next morning with a feeling of dread. Last night, I didn't have a single dream. My heart was racing, and I tuned my ears, listening for any sounds of danger. Nothing.

I got out of bed and got dressed, grabbing my magic flashlight from my bedside table, and walked downstairs. It was Saturday, so I didn't have any classes, so I left my backpack sitting on the chair in the common room.

When I opened the door to the stairs, Rob was standing there, his hand raised, ready to knock.

"What's up?" I asked.

"Leo wants to see us after breakfast." He said.

"Did he say why?"

Rob shook his head.

"Just said we needed to meet him in his office after we eat."

"Did he ask anyone else to come?" I questioned as we walked down the stairs.

"All of our friends." He explained. "You, me, Rachael, Blake, Megan, and Penny."

"I wonder why."

Rob and I walked into the dining hall and took our seats. Everyone was already seated, and there was an air of tension throughout the room. We all ate in silence. Every now and then, Penny would look over at me and smile, but so would Rachael. I then remembered that Rachael and I had planned this afternoon to go into Erie and to be honest, I was kind of excited to hang out with her and get off the school grounds for a while.

Once we had finished eating, Leo looked at my friends and me.

"Please meet me in my office immediately." He ordered and left the table.

My friends and I got up and followed Leo out of the dining hall, quietly discussing what was going on. When we entered Leo's office, however, we fell silent. Leo had a grave look on his face. Six chairs were sitting in front of his desk.

"Please, sit," Leo instructed, so we did.

"What's up, sir?" Rob asked, leaning his chair back so it stood on only two legs.

"Well, first things first, thank you all for meeting with me." Leo started, taking a breath. "Secondly, I have a very important mission for all of you."

My friends and I exchanged looks. From what I've been told, most missions and quests were done by three people, not six.

"I've received word from Hermes, that there is an attacked being planned. Hermes had intercepted a message coming from somewhere out west, though he is not sure of its origin. However, from the direction it was coming, it seemed to be from Mount Saint Helens." Leo explained.

Rachael and Megan gasped. Penny and Blake both had hard looks on their faces. Rob was just shaking his head.

"What's in Mount Saint Helens? Isn't that a volcano?" I asked, slightly confused.

"Well, it's hard to explain, Jensen. First, you need to understand something." Leo started. "The gods live where they have the biggest following, where people believe in them the most, or honor them the most. Right now, that place is in America. From our architecture to the statues and symbolism, the United States has the highest concentration of influence."

I nodded, trying to follow along.

"Right now, Olympus is located in the place where people hold the most power, Washington D.C.."

"Okay," I said.

"The Underworld moves just as Olympus. It is always located in a very unpopulated area, somewhere dangerous to go. In this case, it is located below Mount Saint Helens in Washington state."

"Okay, so let me get this straight. Mount Olympus is located somewhere in Washington D.C.-"

"Specifically, about three miles above the Washington Monument. Invisible to mortals." Rachael interrupted.

"Right," I said. "So Olympus is in D.C., and the Underworld is at the bottom of an active volcano."

"Correct," Leo said. "It's actually far below the mountain, but the only entrance is through the mouth of the volcano."

"Awesome," I said sarcastically.

"Now, the reason I bring this up is that the message that was intercepted was information on a battle plan."

Rachael and Blake moved to the end of their chairs.

"It seems, Hades is planning an attack on our school."

"Why?" Rachael asked, with a look of horror on her face.

"Well, it seems, because of Jensen," Leo explained to us.

There was silence in the room for a few moments. Rob had returned his chair to all fours, and he was looking at me, worry on his face.

"Me? Why me?" I was so confused.

Leo took a deep breath.

"Jensen, I feel sure that you know the story of the first werewolves."

"Of course. Zeus created them after Lycaon tried to feed him one of his children for dinner." I said.

Leo nodded.

"Well, after that Zeus made a decree that no god shall be involved with a werewolf. He made all the gods swear on the River Styx, which is a binding oath, the most sacred. Breaking the oath, results in, well, extremely bad things, to say the least. Because you are sitting here, Jensen, you know Zeus himself, broke this oath."

I looked at Leo for a few moments, in sort of shocked silence.

"So what does this mean?" I finally asked him.

"It means, that Hades is not happy. He believes that you should not be alive, and he will try very hard to make it so you are not. He seems to be sending an army, in seven days."

No one said a word, but everyone was looking at me. Rachael and Penny looked as if they were punched in the stomach. After about a minute of this, Leo cleared his throat and began speaking again.

"Now, we, that is to say, I, have a plan to ensure this attack does not happen. Hence, why you are all here. We're going to stop the attack before it even happens."

"What are we going to do?" Rachael asked Leo.

"You six, are going to enter the Underworld, and sabotage Hades army before it can be deployed," Leo answered.

I had to speak up.

"But, doesn't that play right into what Hades wants? He wants me dead, and I would be walking right to him."

"This is true. However, you are our greatest weapon. Hades would not expect you of all people to come and face him. Besides, if all goes according to plan, he would not even know you were there until you were gone."

"What is this plan?" I asked.

"Simple. You enter the Underworld quietly. You plant charges of greek fire, the most deadly incendiary device in creation, around Hades' army camp, prime detonators, and leave. Many monsters would be lost, and they would take enough time to reform for us to receive assistance from Olympus once they have held a council."

"What if we get caught?" Rachael questioned.

"If that happens, that is why Jensen is going to join you. You fight back, and escape."

It sounded pretty insane to me. Enter an active volcano, blow up an army of monsters, and escape back to school. All in seven days. I gripped my flashlight in my pocket, running my fingers down it.

"Well," I said, after about three minutes of silence. "Sounds like we have a job to do, as long as everyone's on board." I looked around at my friends, who were also looking at me.

One by one, they all nodded in agreement.

"Good," Leo said. "This needs to take place as quickly as possible. Now, on the downside, Hermes has not granted us quick travel this time around so it will take you a while to get there. I require you to pack supplies and leave. I will provide a travel plan to Rachael."

"Who's in charge?" Penny asked, looking Leo right in his shining blue eyes.

"That would be you, my dear," Leo answered. "You may pick your own second, as always."

Penny nodded.

"Now, please, go and prepare," Leo said, standing up from his desk. "Rachael, please, after you have gathered your things, meet me back here for the travel plans."

Rachael nodded as we all got up. When we were finally outside Leo's office, Penny gathered us around her, in sort of a huddle.

"First things first. Rachael, you're my second." Penny said. "Second, I need everyone to meet me back here in twenty minutes. You heard Leo, we have to leave as soon as possible."

We all agreed.

To speed things along, at the bottom of the stairs, I used the winds to move everyone to their dorms. It was a lot harder to lift people when I wasn't carrying them, but I managed.

When I got to my dorm, I grabbed my backpack off the chair in the common room. I emptied my books on to the coffee table and ran to my room. Reaching into my dresser, I pulled out two more pairs of jeans, a few shirts, socks, and underwear. I pulled my fingerless gloves from my nightstand and put them on.

Then, I remembered something. I opened up my sock drawer again and picked up the pair that held the money I received from my uncle on my birthday. A thousand dollars was still sitting there. I didn't think I needed it all, so I pulled out five hundred and put it inside one of the pockets in my backpack.

Once I had everything packed up and ready to go, I checked my watch and saw that I still had five minutes to meet everyone else. I jumped down from my landing, and let the winds carry me down to the ground floor. Rob was waiting by the entrance hall doors. He motioned me over.

"Ready?" I asked him.

He nodded and opened his pack. Rob handed me a bedroll, and sheath for my sword.

"Figured you wouldn't have a bedroll, and needed somewhere to put your sword for easy access."

"Thanks," I said, putting the bedroll in my backpack and strapping the sheath to my side.

We waited there together in silence for another few minutes. Rachael walked out of Leo's office, map in hand, right when everyone else was descending the stairs. They all converged with Rob and me.

"Everyone ready?" Penny asked.

We all nodded.

"Right," Rachael said, "We have no transport, so most of it's going to be on foot unless we want to go to the ocean and have some help from Penny's dad."

"No," Penny said with authority.

"Okay, so walking it is." Rachael continued. "We'll head west, keeping close to the north." She was holding up the map and showing us.

"How long of a walk is that?" Rob asked.

"Normally, about a month. However, I know someone in Cleveland that can help us. It's about a day and a half walk. From there, I'd say that it would take us a day. Leonardo said we only have seven days. So we don't have a lot of room for error." Rachael explained.

"Alright," Penny started. "Formation goes as follows: Blake on point, Rob, Jensen, Me, Rachael, Megan. Megan will provide covering fire in case of an attack. Jensen will periodically take to the air, and give us a sitrep. Straight line, heads on a swivel. Understood?"

Again, we all agreed.

"Let's get going then."

Blake led us out of the front gates, and we started heading through the forest. We didn't do much talking to start off with, we were all stuck in our own thoughts. Mine was primarily focused on Hades and the treaty that my father broke. I looked up into the sky, thinking hard. Why would he break the oath, if he didn't really love my mother? If he did he would have stuck around. Or, maybe he did love my mother but didn't love me. So many feelings were going through me, I didn't know what to do.

After about an hour into our walk, Penny instructed me to take to the air. I broke the tree line and raised about a hundred more feet in the air. When I focused my eyes, I saw a small group about two hundred yards to our right, still in the woods, but just barely. I smelled the air and picked up a burning scent.

I hit the ground again and shared this with Penny and the others.

"Burning? Probably hellhounds." Penny said.

"I couldn't get a good view of them, but they did look pretty big. There were about ten of them." I added.

"Alright, we'll move farther left, and try to avoid them."

We did just that and kept an even pace. I kept my ears and nose at the ready, but nothing came just then. As we walked, I took to the air about every half an hour to check our surroundings.

Once, as I broke the tree line, I caught the scent of werewolves again. The same, old, powerful scent as before. This time, it was closer. Maybe only a hundred feet away.

When I hit the ground, I was in some sort of trance. I felt eyes on me from the distance. I looked around but saw nothing. Some sort of force was trying to pull me further into the forest, away from my friends. Fighting the urge, I kept walking after Penny poked me in the back with the butt of her sword.

"You okay?" She asked, sounding worried.

"Fine," I responded.

After about six more hours of constant walking, I rose above the trees a final time. The sun was still high in the air, I checked my watch, and it was only a little after three. When I reached a suitable altitude, I looked around, and what I saw did not please me.

To my right, about half a mile away, on the edge of Lake Erie, surrounded by cliffs and sharp rocks, were six monsters. They were drinking from the lake. The monsters had the body, hind legs, and tail of a lion. In the front, they had what seemed to be eagle feet and talons, and an eagle's head and wings. Giant wings. The creatures themselves were at least ten feet long. They looked up from their drink, and one of them caught my eye. I heard it let out a blood-curdling shriek, like a normal eagle call, but sharper.

I raced toward the ground and informed my friends of the situation.

"What?! Griffins?" Rachael said, putting away her map and pulling out her sword and shield.

I tuned my ears and heard the flapping of massive wings.

"They're coming. I'll head them off." I said.

"Agreed. Megan, get to the top of a tree and support him. Everyone else will stay here and take them when they get close to the ground." Penny ordered.

We all agreed, and I took to the air as Megan ran for the tallest tree. When I was about two hundred feet in the air, I saw the griffins flying towards me. I pulled my flashlight out of my pocket and dropped my backpack to the ground. I heard the soft thump when it hit the ground.

The Griffins were about a hundred yards away from me. Right below me, I saw Megan's head pop out of the trees, her bow at the ready. I quickly turned my flashlight into a sword and raised it, pointing it at the first Griffin. Summoning lightning from the sky, I sent a bolt straight at the Griffin.

Before it could react, the bolt of lightning hit the Griffin in the chest, it burst into flames instantly. The other five griffins, however, simply flew around their departed ally and flew straight at me. I dodged the first and sliced at it with my sword, but the griffin grabbed it in its claws. My sword slipped out of my hand, the Griffin still clutching it in its claws.

The next two monsters came at me, but I wasn't as quick this time, still focusing on the one that stole my sword. One of the griffins sank it's talons into my side, the other, into my arm. I screamed in pain, as an arrow caught one of the griffins holding me in the head. I felt the warmth of the flames as the monster dissipated. However, there were still talons in my arm. I extended my claws and slashed at its torso, and it burned away.

I felt my wounds healing slowly. They were pretty deep.

The griffin holding my sword was now plummeting to the ground. I summoned a bolt of lightning from inside of me and sent it straight toward the creature. My aim was slightly off, but I did manage to clip its wing, and it dropped my sword as it fell to the ground. I summoned the weapon back to my hand using the winds.

I caught it right when the last two griffins were feet from me. Transforming my sword into a shield with a quick shock of electricity, I blocked both sets of talons that were seconds away from entering my chest. Using the winds, I flew a few feet back while simultaneously changing my sword to a spear.

In one fluid motion, I swiped with my spear, catching both griffins in the chest. They burst into flames as the pain in my chest and arm finally got to me. I looked down and noticed a lot of blood pouring from my wounds. They were still healing, but not as quickly as they normally should have. I lost control of the winds and dropped like a bullet to the ground.

I woke up a few minutes later, the holes in my arm and chest fully healed. Penny was feeding me ambrosia. It tasted like chocolate cake with strawberry icing; my favorite. Propping myself up on my elbows, I looked around. Penny and Rachael seemed glad I was awake and moving. To my left, about twenty feet away, there was a human-sized crater about five feet deep. I had a dull pain in my ribs like they had broken but healed recently.

"So, I take it I fell?" I asked Penny, who was putting her ambrosia back into her bag.

"Yeah. How you're not dead, I have no idea, you seemed to have lost a lot of blood from the looks of your clothes."

"My wounds took longer than I thought they would too heal. You have any ideas why?" I questioned as I got to my feet and took off my shirt.

"It might be that creatures that can fly do more damage to you. Sea monsters normally do more damage to me, even if I'm in the water and can heal quickly." Penny explained to me.

"Makes sense." I pulled a fresh shirt out of my backpack and put it on. "What happened to the last griffin?"

"It hit the ground but didn't make it much further. Blake stabbed it in the back."

"Nice."

I walked over to where my spear lay, next to the crater I had made, and picked it up, turned it into a sword again, and placed it in the sheath that Rob had given me.

"We're camping here," Rachael said, walking up to me and putting her hand on my shoulder.

I checked my watch and saw that it was only about four o clock.

"Are you okay?" Rachael asked me.

"Yeah, I'm fine. I'm just curious as to why we're stopping. We could still keep walking. It's not going to be dark for another five hours at least."

"We figured it was best. We've already been walking for seven hours. After you got hurt, we wanted to give you a little more time to heal. You hit the ground pretty hard." Rachael explained, taking her hand off of my shoulder.

"I'm fine. Really. My ribs are healed, and my wounds from the fight are gone." I pulled up my shirt and showed her my chest where the wounds had been.

Her face turned a deep shade of red.

"I know, but better safe than sorry." She said, her voice seemed to have gone up an octave.

"Sorry," I said, lowering my shirt.

"It's okay. Let's go sit down, Rob made a fire, we'll get something to eat."

Rachael and I walked over to where Rob and Penny were sitting. A fire was roaring in a homemade fire pit Rob had dug, and there was some kind of meat cooking over top of it.

"What's that?" I asked Rob as I sat down in between Rachael and Penny on a tree stump.

"Venison. I got some from the kitchens at school. I made a special pouch in my bag that will keep it cold and fresh." Rob told me, flipping one of the steaks.

As we ate, we were mostly silent. Rachael kept giving Penny and me weird looks. Every now and then, I would tune my ears to try and pick up any signs of incoming monsters, but nothing seemed to be incoming. All I heard was Rachael's heartbeat increasing every so often.

"I think about an hour after it gets dark, we should get moving again. How are you feeling, Jensen?" Penny said once everyone had eaten.

"I've felt fine. We really didn't have to stop at all." I told her.

"It was for the best," Rachael said, cutting off Penny as she opened her mouth to talk. "We'd rather you be fully healed."

"You guys always forget, I heal quick." I joked.

Rachael and Penny were still looking at each other.

"Anyway," Rob said, breaking the tension. "That sounds good Penny."

I checked my watch, it was a little past five now.

"I'll keep watch, you guys should get some rest. I'll wake you up when it's dark." I said.

They all agreed and started pulling out their bedrolls from their bags. Blake extinguished the fire, and Megan picked up the food scraps and paper plates leftover from our meal.

Once everyone was asleep, I pulled out my sword and jumped up into the tallest tree I could find, while still keeping an eye on everyone on the ground.

While I was sitting there, I thought about everything. My mother, my father, the gods, and the adventure ahead of us. Why had my father not stayed with my mother? Had he really not loved her? My thoughts from earlier coming back. Then I stopped for a second. Of course, he loved her. Why would he break that oath if he didn't? He barely knew I existed, so it couldn't have been because of me.

Then again, he is the god of all gods, and it's not like my mother had a hard life. She was the alpha of our pack. We never struggled with money. Maybe him leaving wasn't that bad after all. Would things really have been different if he popped in every now and then? Probably not, besides the fact I would have known I was a demigod a little bit sooner. It's not like Zeus and I would have played catch outside every other weekend or anything.

Of course, there was this quest that we were on to blow up a potential army. Why couldn't the other gods just take care of it? Why did they have to have a council to discuss it? It didn't make any sense. These are all-powerful beings were talking about. Now, granted, I've never met any of them, but they shouldn't have to have meetings to stop their children from dying.

My friends and I are going to risk our lives, to save everyone else. All the gods had to do is wave a hand, and the threat would be gone. It didn't make any sense to me.

As if my thoughts were permeating through the forest, I heard the branches beneath me move. A few seconds later, Rachael was sitting on a branch next to me.

"I couldn't sleep, thought you'd like some company." She said with a smile.

"I wouldn't mind it," I told her, which was true, I never minded Rachael's company.

"So, what are you doing?" She asked.

"Thinking," I said and told her what was on my mind about the quest.

She took a few moments before saying anything, probably picking her words carefully.

"You see Jensen, the gods work weirdly." She started. "They can't just go around using their power to stop another god from doing something. They need to make sure it's the best decision for all of Olympus. They use their children as tools most of the time. Demigods are generally better in making quick decisions because our power can't normally change the entire world."

"That still doesn't seem right to me."

"Jensen, except for a few, like some presidents and kings and whatnot, most demigods can just do things without worrying about the outcome. The gods send us to do things. Like our quest for example." She paused again for a few seconds. "They're sending us because if we die, then they know they need to intervene. It gives them more information. However, if we succeed, then they don't need to do anything. At least not right now."

"That seems really selfish. They don't even care about their children." I grumbled.

"Yes, they do. It's just, the gods control the entire world. One wrong move, an entire country could be destroyed."

I nodded, still in my own thoughts. It was a few more minutes before Rachael spoke again.

"I'm sorry we couldn't go on our date." She said finally. She was blushing when I looked at her. She blushed a lot.

I'm an idiot. Of course, our plans for today were a date.

"Yeah, me too. I was looking forward to it." I offered, and in all honesty, I was.

"Maybe, when we get back, we could actually have it." She responded.

"I'd like that a lot."

Rachael looked at me for a few seconds before doing anything. Her blushing was becoming a deeper shade of red.

"Anyway," I said, mainly to break the tension. I checked my watch, and it had been about three hours since everyone went to sleep. The sun was starting to go down.

"I think we should wake everyone up, break camp and get ready to move," I told Rachael.

She agreed and climbed down the tree. I waited a few moments before following her.

When we were back on the ground, Penny was already awake, looking at us while rolling up her bedroll. Everyone else was up a few moments later and started to break camp.

Once we were all packed up, we started walking again. This part was a bit more difficult because we didn't have a large stretch of forest to walk through, we'd have to go along the roads. Most of the time, we were able to avoid a lot of traffic and people. Every now and then, however, we came across groups of people, and every time, I would tune my hearing and sense of smell, keeping a lookout for more monsters.

We walked without any incidents all night, and the sun rose into the sky. Another eight hours of walking. Fifteen hours total, we were about halfway there. Penny decided that we should make camp for a while, get some more rest and something to eat.

There was a small diner down the road, so we decided to stop there and eat. We hid all of our weapons that we could in our bags and left our shields outside. I turned my sword back into a flashlight and stashed it in my pocket.

Now, from what Rachael explained to me, regular people, mortals, can't normally see our weapons. Apparently, when a child of Hephaestus makes a weapon, there's some sort of magic that goes on that hides it from them. The same thing goes for monsters and whatnot, most of the time. There really isn't a name for it, but my friends just refer to it as the Magic. However, it's still different than regular magic, like the kids in the Hecate dorm used, since their mom was the goddess of magic.

We walked into the restaurant and got seated in the back, where we could see the front door. Our waitress sat us in a booth, so Rachael, Penny, and I took the side facing the door. When we gave our drink order, I opened my bag and took my money out.

"Get whatever you guys want. It's on me." I told my friends.

They must have ordered half the menu. There were pancakes, bacon, sausage, home fries. I ordered a country fried steak with sausage gravy. We sat there and ate, but didn't talk much. I didn't realize how hungry I was after walking all night.

The restaurant was pretty empty. Three men were sitting towards the front, sitting on stools at a counter. Every so often, I would notice they were staring at us, however, I didn't pick up any weird scent. The man that was staring at us the most had a scar going over his eye, and down his face. I pointed them out to Rachael, who was on my left.

She looked over at them when they weren't looking.

"I don't think they're a monster." She whispered to me. "Let's just eat, and see if they follow when we leave."

I agreed and continued to eat my country fried steak.

We finished eating and got our check. It was a little over fifty dollars. I left a hundred on the table, and we gathered our things and left, me in the back, Blake in the front.

When we were outside and gathered our shields, we walked a few hundred feet down the road. I kept my hearing and smell on high alert, trying to pick up a sign of anyone following us. For now, it seemed we were in the clear.

Up ahead on the side of the road, there was a small motel. I offered to pay again, that way we could have a good night's sleep in an actual bed before the rest of our journey. The others protested, but I insisted.

I got two rooms with two beds each. It was only about sixty dollars a room, not bad. Our rooms were side by side. Blake, Megan, and Rachael took one room, Penny, Rob and I took the other. I guess Blake and Rachael wanted to spend some time planning the rest of our mission before they slept. It was fine with me, the more planning done, the better our chances are to survive.

We all went to our rooms, it was around eight o clock by the time we all got into bed. The rooms only had two beds. Rob said he kicks in his sleep. So Penny and I let him take the one bed, and we took the other with a wall of pillows between us.

When we fell asleep, I was almost instantly dropped into a dream.

I was standing on the top of a mountain. No, not a mountain, a volcano. There was lava flowing right under my feet, about three feet to my right. In front of me stood a man in long black robes with what looked like faces sewn into the fabric. He had a black sword, at least five feet long, in his hand. The man's hair was shoulder-length, dark brown, with grey streaks. His eyes and beard resembled black fire.

The man motioned to the volcano.

"This, Jensen Smith will be where you die." He said with a booming voice that radiated power.

The wind started to billow around us, tossing the man's robes and hair.

"If you continue with this quest, this is your fate!"

The man raised his sword and slashed it in my direction.

I awoke with a start, just a small little twitch. After lying there a few moments, I noticed that Penny had rolled over the pillow wall and had her arm lying on my chest. Rob was sitting on the edge of his bed, having just woken up, and was staring at us.

"What's up?" He whispered with a smile.

I slowly moved Penny's arm off of my chest, grabbed a shirt, put my watch on, and walked outside with Rob. Checking my watch, it was three in the afternoon.

"So, what was that about?" Rob asked, closing the door behind us.

"Not now, I need to tell you something."

I told Rob of my dream of the man. After I was done, Rob just looked at me for a minute before speaking.

"Dude, I'm pretty sure you just had a dream about Hades."

"Why would I dream about him?" I asked.

"Sometimes, from what I've heard, Hades can penetrate people's dreams. From what you described, it sounds a lot like him. I've only met him once, but you've got it about right."

"You think we should tell everyone else?"

Rob nodded.

"Especially Megan, her dad's the god of prophecy, she might have an insight." He said.

Once everyone had woken up, we met in Rachael's room, where our map was sitting on one of the beds.

I told everyone about my dream.

"I think," Megan started, "that this would mean you're going to have a confrontation with Hades. He likes to threaten everyone with death."

"Well, he's a god, I'm pretty sure he can kill anyone he wants," I said.

"Yes, but you're a child of Zeus. If he kills you, whether he's met you or not, Zeus would wage war on the Underworld, he won't wait for the council of gods to decide."

"I guess I've got that goin' for me. All I have to do is let Hades kill me, and then no more threats to the school." I joked.

Rachael and Penny looked absolutely terrified for me.

"I'm kidding," I reassured them, they didn't look it. "I promise. We should get going."

We packed up all of our things, I paid the lady at the front desk and started walking down the street. It was about five o'clock now. We still had about fifteen more hours of walking ahead of us.

After we walked another mile, I heard a low growl off to our right, just inside a tree line.

Out of the trees, stepped a man with a leather jacket on, and a scar across his face. The same man I had seen at the diner.

"I can't let you go any further." He said in a thick ancient accent.

"Who are you?" I asked him, stepping forward, my hand in my pocket.

The man now had a grin on his face.

"I, son of Zeus, am Damysus, and I have excellent hearing."

9

Chapter Nine: The world's fastest giant

"Who in Hades is Damysus?" I asked.

"Let me show you," Damysus said and started to grow.

His arms and legs started to enlarge, then his torso, and finally, his head. Before long, there was the man with the scar on his face, the same leather jacket, but he was at least twenty feet tall. I looked up at him in amazement. Looking around, I saw no mortals on the street, and I heard no cars coming.

"Jensen," Rachael whispered, putting her hand on my shoulder to get my attention.

"What?" I whispered back.

"We should run. Damysus is the fastest giant that ever lived."

"You got that right!" The giant yelled at us. "I heard your talk in the motel. You're not

going to make it to the Underworld."

Before I could do anything, the giant moved. I barely saw him. He ran straight at me and kicked me square in the chest. I went flying across the road and through some trees. Finally, I hit the ground about two hundred feet away.

I got up with weak knees. A few of my ribs were broken. When I got to my feet, I could hear sounds of battle coming from the street. I staggered to the tree line, and what I saw blew my mind.

Damysus was running circles, literally, around my friends. He was kicking up a tailwind so strong that I could see debris flying everywhere. Looking through the haze, I could see my friends on their knees, they looked like they were struggling to breathe. Every now and then, I saw one of Damysus' feet or hands make contact with one of my friends, and they were forced to the ground.

I didn't have time to think. Reaching into my pocket, I took my flashlight out and turned it into a shield. I timed it as best I could, and threw my shield towards the giant as hard as I could, which was pretty hard. Luckily, it made contact, and the giant flew back into the trees.

The debris that was soaring around my friends hit the ground. I shifted and extended my claws. My friends were still on the ground, and from what I could see, I had a few cuts and bruises. However, I didn't have time to help them up. Damysus was recovering.

He picked up my shield from beside him and threw it down the street the way we came. It flew for at least a mile. The giant moved with blinding speed, but while I was shifted, I had no problem following his movements. He tried to punch me, but I caught his fist in my hand. I picked him up by the arm. Damysus weighed at least three tons, but that was well within my ability. Putting as much of my strength behind it as I could, I threw the giant two miles down the road.

He hit the ground and it shook like there was a small earthquake. I ran at full speed toward him as he was getting up. When I was thirty feet away, I jumped and brought my claws across the giant's chest. Damysus yelled in pain but didn't burst into flames.

Before I could land, the giant grabbed my left leg and spun me like a windmill into the ground. I felt the rest of my ribs break, along with the leg that Damysus was holding. When he let go of me, I tried to get up, but before I could move, I was punched in the chest by a hubcap-sized fist.

Behind me, I could hear my friends running toward me. I opened my eyes and saw arrows hitting Damysus in the chest. He staggered backward.

I got up onto my knees. I was in so much pain. When I tried to stand, I felt a sharp pain in my side, and collapsed, coughing up blood. A few moments later, somebody was pulling my arm over their shoulders and leading me away.

"It'll be okay." Penny was saying. "We'll get him." She sounded like she was crying.

I gently pushed her away.

"I'll be fine. Go help the others." I told her, and I took my arm from around her shoulders.

"I'm not going to leave you, Jensen." She said, a tear in her eyes. "You're so hurt."

I stood on my own for a few moments. It hurt and I stumbled, but I was able to do it. My ribs were starting to heal, as were the cuts on my face and arms.

"I'm fine. Go." I ordered.

She looked at me for a few moments, then our heads snapped back to the battle.

Damysus had recovered, and my friends were being pushed back. Megan's arrows were being slapped out of the air at blinding speed. Rob and Blake were right in front of the giant, shields up, swords out, stabbing away. However, they weren't doing any damage. The giant seemed to be doing a jig and every sword missed.

Rachael was back with Megan, protecting her with her shield as Megan released arrows.

"Go," I told Penny. "I'm right behind you."

Penny drew her sword, took her shield off her back and ran into battle.

I staggered for a few moments, hoping my bones would heal quickly, but they were taking a while. However, I couldn't leave my friends without help.

I looked down the street and saw the light shining off of my shield. Channeling a wind current, I picked my shield up and brought it back to my hand.

Trying to ignore the pain in my chest, I yelled at Damysus.

"Hey, ugly!" The giant kicked Rob and Blake in the shield and they flew backward. His eyes looked directly into mine.

I threw my shield with all my strength. It flew through the air, surprisingly too fast for the giant, and it hit him in the face. Running as quickly as I could, I jumped and grabbed my shield as it bounced off Damysus' nose. As I jumped, I turned my shield into a spear and stabbed the giant in the neck. Silver blood started pouring from the wound, Damysus screamed in pain but managed to swat me out of the air. I flew back but landed in Penny's arms.

"Hey." She said a smile on her face.

"Hi. Um, can you let me down? I've got a giant to kill."

She obliged, and I hit the ground running, but with a slight limp. Damysus still hadn't recovered, blood was still coming from his neck. My spear was still in my hand. As hard as I could, I chucked it into the giant's chest. He grabbed at the spear, trying to pull it out, but it was too deep.

Concentrating as hard as I could with the pain I was in, I summoned a lightning bolt from the sky and sent it to the end of my spear. A few moments later, arcs of electricity were streaming from Damysus' chest.

The giant was yelling in pain. Silver blood was covering the road. As Damysus stumbled around, he fell into some trees, which crumbled on top of him.

"No!" He yelled. "You will not kill me! I will not go back to Tartarus!"

Penny walked calmly past me, sword in hand.

"I don't think you have a choice." She said confidently.

With a strong swipe of her sword, she lopped the giants head off. Once it had stopped rolling, Damysus' body began to burn.

Before anything else could happen, I dropped to the ground, and the world was black. I passed out.

Thankfully, it only lasted a few seconds this time. When I came too, Megan had flipped me on my back and was feeding me ambrosia. She had her medical bag open next to her. When she saw my eyes open, she stopped forcing the medicine into my mouth.

"Are you okay?" She asked, putting the ambrosia away.

I touched my ribs and felt that they were almost fully healed.

"Give me another few minutes and I will be," I told her, slowly sitting up on my elbows.

I looked around and saw that Megan had patched everyone else up as well. Rob and Blake had cuts and bruises all over their faces and arms. Penny had a bandage around her leg. Rachael looked more or less unharmed, aside from a few bruises on her left arm.

"Everyone okay?" I asked.

They all nodded.

"What about you?" Rachael asked concern washed across her face.

"Fine. Feel like I could go another five rounds." I laughed, as I raised to my feet. I winced a little but managed to stay standing.

"We lost about half an hour with that fight," Penny said. "We need to get moving. Sadly, we can't wait for Jensen to heal anymore."

"No worries. I'm fine." I promised.

With Penny's order, we picked up our bags, which we had left in the middle of the road, gathered into formation, and started walking again. Megan said it wasn't a good idea to go too fast since my ribs and leg were still healing, but I protested, and everyone broke into a light jog.

Now, something nice about demigods, especially werewolf demigods, we have great stamina. Normally, I could be in a full sprint, at three hundred miles an hour, for hours. Even with the broken ribs, which were now mostly healed, I was able to jog for what seemed like forever. My friends were able to keep pace, and we had a pretty decent speed for what seemed like two hours. While we went, I wondered how good their stamina would be full-on running.

As we went, I kept checking ahead of us for any threats. Raising into the air about every half an hour like I had done the previous day, I didn't see anything out of the ordinary.

Actually, surprisingly, the rest of the journey went pretty smoothly. We ran into very little obstacles. Once we had to go about a mile out of our way to avoid a group of centaurs; men with the bodies of horses. Other than that, I didn't see any monsters.

After making up the time we spent with the fight by jogging, we slowed into a normal walking pace. I figured we traveled at least five more miles so far. The others were slightly out of breath but were still able to keep going. My ribs and other wounds had healed completely about five minutes into our journey.

It was a little after seven now, and the sun was starting to set, but we still had another hour or so of sunlight. I looked behind me and noticed Megan was staring at the sun. I slowed up a little, and let me Rachael swap me spots.

"You okay?" I asked Megan.

"Yeah, just thinking about my dad."

Megan never really shared stuff with me. We weren't exactly the closest friends, I liked her and everything and we were friends, but we never had one-on-one time.

"Oh," I said, kind of awkwardly.

"I haven't seen him for a few years. That's normal though, but I still kind of miss him sometimes. Especially at sunset."

"I'm sorry," I told her, and I was. I understood what it was like to not have my dad around, obviously.

"It's okay. I'll see him again. If we survive."

"I hope we do," I told her.

"We've got you. It's almost impossible to fail." Rachael said, turning around.

"What do you mean?" I asked her.

"Well, as Leo said, you're our secret weapon. You're the most powerful demigod we have. You were the only one who could do any real damage to Damysus. Most people wouldn't survive combat with a giant."

"Well, if you didn't notice Rachael, I sorta got beat down."

"Yeah, you got beat down by the fastest, and one of the most powerful giants that's ever lived. You survived."

"I guess so."

I didn't feel particularly powerful, but Rachael did make a good point. In the last month at school, I didn't hear about anyone else going toe-to-toe with a giant like that.

Rachael and I switched positions again and kept walking.

We walked straight through the night, and only stopped when the sun was rising again. Penny decided we should stop and eat, due to not having done so for eleven hours. Everyone stopped on the side of the road at a little park with a few benches.

Rob made a small fire from some branches of the trees that were around the park. He cooked up a few venison steaks. As we ate, Rachael filled us in on where we were going.

"Well, this person I know in Cleveland, he should help us." She said.

"Who is it?" Blake asked.

Rachael took a few bites of her steak before speaking.

"A powerful son of Hermes. He can give us passage." She explained.

"How is he going to give us passage to Mount Saint Helens?" I questioned.

"Well, as with all the gods, sometimes they give their children special powers. Most children of Hermes are just really good thieves and are really good with directions. Some get super speed, like Andrew back at school."

I remembered the kid that was sparing with Penny a few weeks ago. He did seem to have god-like speed.

"Anyway." Rachael continued. "Very, very, few children of Hermes, are granted the power to send messages or packages. Kind of like Hermes himself."

"So basically, we're going to be a package." Rob joked.

Rachael nodded.

"How do you know this person? Why haven't we heard of him before?" Blake asked, raising an eyebrow.

"You have. It's my cousin, David."

"Wait, you have a cousin who's a demigod too?" I said, taken aback.

"Yep. He's a little older than us, in his twenties, but he was given that special power by Hermes. He can basically open a portal for us straight to Mount Saint Helens."

"That's awesome!" Blake said, smiling.

Penny didn't look surprised. Because she's Rachael's best friend, I assumed she already knew this information.

"We're going to his warehouse. He runs a shipping company. Having the powers he does, he makes really good money. It takes a lot out of him though. The shipping normally takes the same time as normal, but it's always on time." Rachael informed us.

"Does he have the power to send all of us?" Blake asked. It was a good question.

"I think so. Although, he might have to shut down for the day. It'll probably take everything he has." She answered.

Blake just nodded.

We finished eating and packed everything. Everyone looked tired, but we decided to keep going since we only had about six more hours of walking ahead of us.

Blake took the lead, and we trudged on.

The rest of the journey was uneventful. Lots of walking, lots of cars, and lots of trees on the side of the road. It had started raining while we were walking, and it was coming down hard. We were soaked within minutes, but we kept walking. I used my wristwatch shield as an umbrella. Everyone else, besides Penny, did the same with their shields.

Penny actually seemed to be dry. I questioned her about this because I just noticed it after we had almost finished our journey to Cleveland.

"I can choose to stay dry if I want to. Only in natural water though, like rain, rivers, the sea."

"That's pretty cool" I admitted.

As we kept walking, the downpour turned into a storm. Lightning was striking through the sky. Thunder boomed all around us.

We were clear ahead. I rose into the air and saw no monsters in our path. Rachael had described the warehouse to me. A huge building that filled an entire city block. It was plain white stone bricks. A big sign was on the front right above the delivery doors. It read: Sage Shipping.

The building was about ten blocks away, and we had just entered the city. Traffic was racing all around us. I hit the ground and told Rachael how far away we were. She shared a look with Penny.

"We should stick to the alleys," Penny said.

"I agree. Due to the power and demigods that are gathered there, monsters tend to hang around. My cousin only hires demigods to work for him. Easier that way. Plus, it's a big city, monsters tend to gather in bigger cities." Rachael shared.

"I didn't see any monsters," I said.

"They can hide pretty well. That's not surprising."

"Why stick to the alleys then?" Megan asked, and she had a good point. Blake answered.

"If we have the get into a fight, we're less likely to be seen in the alleys. The Magic will hide the monsters from mortals, but it might look like we're attacking some animals or something. Plus, we would have more cover, and fewer enemies coming at us at once in a small space."

So, we continued, following the alleys the remaining ten blocks. After a few minutes, we were only one block away. We passed a condemned building with nothing but broken windows and graffiti. From the building, I heard a very sharp hiss. Immediately, I pulled my sword from its sheath and held it at the ready.

Standing in one of the windows was a woman with long black hair and blood-red eyes. Rachael almost ran into me when I stopped, then she saw what I was looking at. The creature's eyes instantly turned to her, and it smiled. Long fangs were in the place of the creatures canine teeth, just like mine, besides the fact that the woman's fangs were much longer.

Rachael pulled her sword from her side as well.

"Mormo." She whispered. "Vampiric demon spirit."

"So, a vampire?"

Rachael didn't have a chance to answer. The mormo jumped from the window. I was ready to defend, but I didn't get the opportunity.

Out of nowhere, a bronze arrow flew towards the demon, striking it directly where its heart should have been. The mormo instantly burst into flames. I spun around to see where the arrow had come from.

I felt a burst of air blow past me and saw a man with short blonde hair, and a dimpled chin. He was a little taller than me. The man carried a bow and had a quiver across his back.

"David!" Rachael yelled, wrapping her cousin in a hug.

"What's up, cuz?" David said, hugging Rachael back. "I saw that mormo coming after you. They like to hang out in that building sometimes."

"Thanks," Rachael said.

"Where'd you guys come from? You didn't say you were coming Rachael."

"We're on a quest. We were wondering if we could get your help."

David had a big smile on his face.

"Let's go in and talk about it. Maybe get you guys something to eat."

David led us into the warehouse through the delivery doors. Inside, conveyor belts were crisscrossing the entire facility. Forklifts were picking up packages and putting them on large sets of shelves that reached the entire way to the ceiling, which was around a hundred feet above my head.

Employees were walking all around, and almost all of them had a weapon secured to their bodies. Then I remembered Rachael said all of Davids staff were demigods, and that monsters like to converge here, due to there being so many demigods in one place. Every employee had a grey collared shirt on with the Sage Shipping logo on it; to S's separated by a staff with two snakes curling around it. The symbol of Hermes.

David led us through the break room at the back of the warehouse, and up a set of steps into his office. It was normal enough. There was a big desk in the middle of the room, with a leather chair behind it. There was a mini-fridge in the corner of the room, and two leather couches on either wall, a glass coffee table in between.

"Take a seat," David said, motioning to the couches.

We took our seats, Penny, Rachael and I on the couch on the right, and Blake, Megan, and Rob on the one on the left. David took his spot behind his desk, still smiling.

"What can I do for you, Rachael?"

"Well, we need a portal, Dave."

David looked a Rachael for a few seconds, considering.

"And where will you need to go?"

"Mount Saint Helens."

David scrunched his eyebrows together.

"You're going to the Underworld? You must be crazy."

"If we don't go, the schools going to be destroyed," Penny answered.

"Hades is sending an army to attack us. It will be deployed in five days. We have to destroy it." Blake added.

David considered this for a moment. Looking at all of us in turn. I wondered what he was thinking.

"As you know Rachael, I love that school. It helped me hone my powers, and gave me a place to go when I had nowhere else. With that being said, I don't want to send my favorite cousin to certain death."

Rachael didn't say anything right away. She sort of just glared at David.

"David. If you don't help us, there is no way we will make it in time. It's either you help us, or all of our friends die."

"Rachael, it's a deathwish. Sending you there would be just as bad as pulling out my sword and killing you myself." Davids' eyes narrowed, a frown on his face.

"Isn't that what Aunt Kim thought when she sent you to school? I remember my dad telling me she was scared you would get killed. She sent you anyway, and everything worked out. How do you know this won't work out?" Rachael rebutted.

Rachael's heartbeat was steady, from what I heard, but she had a scared look on her face. She knew what we were doing could get her killed, but if it meant saving everyone else, she was willing to make the sacrifice, just like everyone else that was on this quest.

Before David could respond, there was a gigantic bang that came from the warehouse. Rachael's cousin pressed a button on his desk, and the desktop turned into a computer monitor that was showing security footage of the warehouse. My friends and I got up and ran over to see what was happening.

On the screen, we saw several bad things. First, one of the warehouse doors had been blown open, and metal was scattered across the floor. Second, several dozen demigods were laying on the ground, blood pouring from their necks. Finally, we saw conveyor belts and forklifts flying through the air, however, we saw no attackers.

"Mormo. They don't appear in the film." David said. "Tell you what. If you help me fight them off, I'll send you anywhere you want."

"Deal." We all said as we drew our weapons.

David led the way down the steps and through the break room. What we saw when we entered the warehouse was worse than what we saw in the security footage. Hundreds of mormo were attacking the demigods. They were fighting back as best as they could, but they were still trying to regroup after the surprise.

Greek Fire bombs were going off all around the facility. Green flames were raging everywhere. Rob was the first to speak.

"Children of Hephaestus. I'll go help them."

He ran off past the conveyor belts into battle.

The rest of us ran in to help everyone else. I noticed a few children of Ares locked in battle, and holding their own. Blake slowed down to help push back the ten demons they were fighting. Megan had broken off and climbed a set of shelves. About halfway up, she stopped and started firing off arrows with expert marksmanship.

David turned on his superspeed and raced off to fight a large group that was closing in on a few of his workers that were wearing hard hats.

"Rachael, go help him. Penny and I will help everyone else."

Rachael nodded and ran after her cousin.

I looked around and saw destruction everywhere. Out of the corner of my eye, I saw water pipes that were running across the ceiling.

"Penny!" I yelled over the roar of the battle. I pointed up to the pipes.

"Throw me!" She yelled back.

I picked her up and shot put her towards the ceiling. She grabbed one of the bigger pipes and sliced it with her sword. Water instantly started gushing out onto the floor. Penny road the current down to the ground, and channeled the water into a group of mormo that were charging us. The force of the blast instantly turned the demons into flames.

Another large group, at least fifty of them, were now coming straight at me. I transformed my sword into a spear and threw it into the middle of the pack. Summoning electricity from my body, I arched a bolt of lightning into my spear, and more arcs stemmed from its contact point. The attack took out at least half of the group.

The others were closing in, however. Using the winds, I summoned my spear back to my hand. As I did so, I pressed the button on my watch and turned it into a shield. Just in time. A mormo had just jumped, it's fangs aiming for my neck. Changing my spear back into a sword the second I caught it, I stabbed the demon in the side, and it evaporated into flames.

After that, I went on autopilot, except for checking on Penny every few moments, I was a battle machine. Any monster in my way was cut down by my sword or claws, which I had extended when I went on the offensive.

At one point a mormo had taken a bite of my leg. Ignoring the pain, I crushed the monster with my shield and kept going. The wound would have been bad on a regular person, but my werewolf physiology healed it within seconds.

While I fought, lightning, fire, and water flew through the air. Monsters were being destroyed at a great rate. I saw Rachael and David at one point. David was literally running a circle around a large group of enemies, kicking up a cyclone. Rachael was stabbing the ones that managed to get through. When I checked on Penny again, Rob and Blake had met with her and they were taking down enemies.

After what seemed like only a few minutes, I heard a blood-curdling screech, and the mormo started to retreat. The fifty or so that were left started pouring out of the destroyed warehouse door. I made to run after them, but Penny grabbed my shoulder.

"Let them go. It's not worth it." I looked around and saw the carnage of the battle. Several dozen demigods lay on the ground. Tuning my hearing, I could catch their heartbeats. No deaths from what I could tell.

My friends and I helped with the cleanup. I carried the forklifts back to the front of the warehouse. Rob and I worked on repairing the conveyor belts. I held them in place while he and a few of his siblings that worked there secured them. The fires were extinguished, and the wounded were given medical attention, aided by Megan.

Once we were done, which took a lot less time than I thought it would, David invited us back to his office. We all sat down once we were inside.

"I owe you guys. Without you, I don't know what would have happened. We were definitely overwhelmed."

"No problem," Blake said.

David looked at me, a curious look on his face.

"Werewolf and a son of Zeus?" He asked me.

"Yup. Hence why Hades wants to attack the school."

David nodded.

"Well. We had a deal, did we not?" David asked Rachael.

Rachael smiled.

"Now, as I'm sure you know, I am not my father. Which means, my powers have limits. The top of the volcano has very strong magical protection, that no one but a god can break. I can only send you to the base of the mountain."

"That would be more than enough," I said.

David shot me a few sharp looks.

"Son of Zeus. I know of the treaty. The one your father has broken."

I didn't say anything. Rachael looked beyond angry.

"I do not condone what you are doing, cousin," David said, addressing Rachael. "Entering the Underworld is more than a deathwish. I only assist you due to your acts today, and the fact that you are family."

"Thank you," Rachael said through gritted teeth.

"Son of Zeus, I hope you live a long, prosperous, life. However, I do not foresee this coming to pass. If Hades wants you dead, chances are, you die."

Again, I said nothing. I had no idea what to say.

David pressed a button on his desk.

"Please bring up the supplies." He said into an intercom.

A few moments later, a couple of Davids employees came in. They carried in bags of supplies. When my friends and I looked through them, we saw food, ambrosia, other medical supplies, and two new quivers filled with arrows for Megan.

"I had them get this ready for you. It's the only other help I can provide." David said.

We split up the food and ambrosia and put them in our bags. Megan swapped the two full quivers, with her now empty one. Once everyone had packed up their things, we all turned to David, who was still sitting behind his desk.

"I wish you luck." He said and snapped his fingers. "I can only keep this open for a few seconds. Sending these many people through at once is going to put me out for a while. I hope you succeed."

To his right, a swirling deep blue portal opened. Through it, I could see a tree-filled forest, and through the clearing, I saw a mountain rise high into the air.

"Thank you again, David," Rachael said and walked through the portal.

My friends and I followed close behind her.

10

Chapter Ten: We enter the Underworld

Traveling through a portal was actually not to bad. To be honest, I didn't even notice it. It was like regular walking, with the exception is that after I stepped through, I was now thousands of miles away.

We walked out into the forest that we had seen through the portal. A few yards in front of us, Mount Saint Helens reached into the sky.

The second we were through, everyone was on high alert. I pulled my sword and pressed the button on my watch. Fine-tuning my hearing, I tried to pick up any signs of monsters. Surprisingly, I heard nothing. Not even normal animals. I shared that with the others.

"Not surprised," Rachael said. "This close to the Underworld, most animals would just die. So they stay away."

"What about the fact that he doesn't hear any monsters?" Rob asked.

"If I were Hades," Blake started. "I would keep all my soldiers in the barracks. Especially since they're only five days away from deployment."

Makes sense. I thought.

"We'll make camp here for a while. Get some sleep. We need it before we infiltrate." Penny ordered.

We pulled our bedrolls from our bags and laid them out. Penny agreed to take the first watch. Before I lay down, I checked my real watch and saw that it was one o'clock eastern time. I rolled it back three hours to match where we were and set an alarm for two hours from now. It made sense for me to take the second watch since I needed less sleep than the rest of my friends.

When I finally fell asleep, there was a problem. A big problem. I didn't dream. I awoke to the sound of my alarm.

I got up and walked over to Penny, who was sitting at the edge of the camp, right by the opening in the trees. She didn't move as I sat next to her.

"Everything okay?" She asked.

"No," I answered.

"Wanna talk about it?"

"I didn't dream. Which is never good." I started and proceeded to tell her why it's not a good thing.

She listened to me and didn't interrupt, which I appreciated. When I was done, she just looked at me for a few moments.

"Well Jensen, the only thing I can say, is to try not to let it bother you. You've got me, and everyone else by your side. We'll make it through this. I'm gonna get some sleep. You gonna be okay?"

I nodded.

"Thanks, Penny."

She got up, placed her hand on my shoulder, and walked over to the camp and lay down.

I sat at the opening of the trees for a few hours. No signs of movement. No threats coming to kill us. I was thankful but then thought about the rest of the mission.

Looking up the mountain, I pictured everything we're going to have to go through. Inside that volcano, was an army of thousands, maybe even millions of monsters, ready to kill us. On top of that, the king of the Underworld, Hades, who hated me for just being alive.

I extended my claws and started making circles in the ground. Wherever my claws went, I saw little puffs of smoke pop from the ground. My best guess was that it was just residual ash or something like that. I looked back up at the mountain, wondering how long it had been since the last eruption. Rachael probably knew the answer to that. She liked looking into national landmarks. Normally, she didn't talk about stuff like that, but she did when we were alone.

The sun went down by the time everyone else had woken up. They needed the sleep, since we went almost a whole day, if not more, without it. I felt fine. Ready to finally enter the Underworld.

Penny was the first one up, and after she lit the fire, she walked over and sat next to me. The sun was about to go down.

"Everything okay?" She asked, sitting next to me again.

"Fine. No signs of anything malicious." I reported.

"We'll make it through this," Penny said, looking me in the eyes.

Apparently, she had seen the look on my face, and it hadn't been a good one.

"I know. Just thinking about everything."

Then she did something very weird. She kissed me on the forehead. That was very un-Pennyish.

"The others are getting up." She told me, looking over at our friends. "Let's make some food, then we can break camp."

Penny got up, and walked over to her bag and started taking food out and putting it into a pot on the fire. She generally wasn't a very emotional person, that's part of what made her a good leader. Normally, emotions were the last thing from her mind, unless there was something deeply troubling to her in the forefront of her mind. Not once, since I've known her, however, had she done something like that.

I looked over at Rachael, who had just gotten off of her bedroll and joined Penny at the fire. She had a look of consternation on her face. I didn't know if that was because of the mission we had ahead of us, or if maybe, she had seen what just happened. After all, we did have a date planned.

I pushed the thought from my mind, I needed to focus on what we were doing. I needed to protect them, and everyone else. After a few moments, I got up but instantly stopped. Again, I felt eyes on me, and that same smell I picked up in the forest at the beginning of our journey.

I was being drawn into the forest again. Something in the back of my mind was telling me to go. My werewolf instincts were kicking in harder than ever before. What was this force that was trying to attract me? I wanted to run into the forest and find whatever it was. I wanted to run free.

"Jensen?" Rob's voice broke into my mind.

I looked down and saw that I had shifted. I haven't shifted without wanting to since I was two.

"Coming," I said, returning to normal, and joining my friends.

After we ate, Penny and Rachael gave us the game plan.

First, we had to climb the mountain. Easy enough. Climb an active volcano. Next, swim through the lava, and reach the entrance. Apparently, a pathway opens up behind you for you to leave from when you reach the doorway to the Underworld. I didn't know who was going for a swim, or how they were going to do it, but I figured, with my healing abilities, it would be me. Finally, once we were inside, navigate Hades realm, find his army, and blow it to kingdom come. Perfectly safe and reasonable plan.

We packed up camp and started up the mountain. This time, we were more spread out, I was on the far left side of the group, Rachael close by. Megan and Blake were taking up the middle, leaving Rob and Penny on the far right. Each one of our groups was about twenty feet apart, making it harder for someone to take us all out if we were attacked. Thankfully though, we met no enemies.

I was happy about this because the walk up the steep mountainside was hard enough. It's not that I lost my balance or anything, but the higher up we climbed, the thinner the air became. About halfway up, Rachael started to slow down. I summoned a wind current from farther down the volcano to give her a little more oxygen. Everyone else seemed to be okay, at least for now.

We started to run into snow a little while after that. Sadly, we had been teleported to the backside of the mountain, which was a whole lot higher than the front. On the plus side, it was almost summer, so there wasn't much snow, just a light dusting. As we walked, I could feel rumbling under my feet. I looked at the others, but they hadn't seemed to notice it. I figured it was just my imagination and kept climbing.

When we had almost reached the top, we ran into a steep section of rocks that went straight to a cliff. No way the others could walk it. I did the only logical thing. I extended my claws.

"Grab on," I told Rachael, and she did, sliding her arms around my neck and propping herself up like she was an oversized backpack.

The others watched as I climbed up the cliff face, sinking my claws deep into the rock. I jumped using the strength in my arms and would clear twenty or thirty feet at a time. Climbing the two hundred feet incline was no problem. Now, the reason I didn't fly everyone up was simple.

Reason number one; carrying that many people on an air current is hard enough in regular conditions, let alone on the top of a mountain with the wind blowing in every direction. I would be lucky to fly myself. Reason number two; it seemed like something was working against me. Like another force that was trying to stop my powers from working.

When I reached the top, Rachael slid off of my back and stood at the top of the mountain.

"Jensen?" She said, but sadly, I had already dropped down the cliff to retrieve the others.

I repeated the process of climbing up the cliff four more times until all of my friends were at the top. Finally, after Penny had slid off my back, I saw what Rachael was trying to show me when I dropped her off.

Below us was an indent in the mountain, and in that indent was a smaller mountain, with a hole in the top, smoke billowing out. The volcano.

Four hundred feet below was a straight drop. To get to the volcano, we'd have to climb back down, then up about two hundred more feet to reach the opening. Doable, however, the rocks we had to climb down seem extremely slick. I got an idea.

"Blake, please tell me you have a spare javelin on you?"

He smiled.

"Of course."

Blake opened his backpack and pulled out a small piece of metal about the size of a pen. He clicked a button on the top, and in his hands, he now held a full two-yard long javelin.

"It's a Rob special." He said as he handed it to me.

"Stand back," I told everyone, and they did, moving as far away from me as possible without falling off the edge.

I reached into my pocket and pulled out my flashlight. With a zap of electricity towards the button, I transformed my light into a spear. Holding the javelin and spear in the air, I summoned two bolts of lightning. They struck with power, almost snapping the javelin in half. I managed to hold the lightning in the tips of the weapons, building up as much extra charge from my body as I could.

Quickly, I pointed the weapons at the rocks twenty feet below us and released the stored plasma in their tips. Lightning arced out in several directions, but I concentrated and kept the blast radius to a minimum. The rocks instantly crumbled.

Granted, it wasn't the best plan, but it seemed to work. The slick rocks below us now turned into decent sized boulders, at least big enough to walk on.

I pressed a button on the side of the javelin and it returned to it's smaller, pen-sized form. Blake placed it back in his bag. I looked at Penny.

"Ladies first?" I joked, motioning to the boulders like a doorman.

She obliged and started jumping from rock to rock. The others followed suit, bouncing around like a group of satyrs. I used the winds and glided down due to the gust being weaker inside the crater. Touching the ground before any of my friends, I walked over the base of the volcano funnel and knelt.

The rocks here were a darker black from centuries of eruptions. They were sharp and harder than any rock I had ever seen. I looked up to where the smoke was coming from, and I remembered my dream.

At the top of this volcano was where Hades said he would kill me. The only difference between my dream and reality was the smoke that was rising into the air. Was this going to be the place where I die? I didn't have much time to ponder it.

My friends had walked up next to me. Penny placed her hand on my shoulder.

"You ready?" She asked, staring up at the smoke.

I got to my feet, and Penny removed her hand.

"Let's do this," I said, transforming my sword back to normal.

As I climbed the rocks, the smoke coming from the volcano grew thicker. It became hard to see. I clicked the light on my flashlight and pointed the beam in front of me so my friends could see. At the same time, I activated my eyes, adding a sky blue glow to the flashlight beam. My infrared vision made it much easier to see.

We reached the top of the funnel a few minutes later. More sharp black rocks lay all over the ground. I looked down into the funnel and saw red-hot lava bubbling a few yards below. My friends were soon by my side, Rachael and Rob looking down. The others were looking around, making sure we were not about to be ambushed.

"Rob?" Rachael said. "You think you can do it?"

I was confused.

"No problem," Rob said, placing his backpack on the ground.

"What are you going to do?"

"Some children of Hephaestus are immune to fire and extreme heat. Rob's one of them."

"So that means you can swim in lava?" I addressed Rob.

"Obviously." He responded with a wink.

A second later, Rob did a backflip into the lava like he was diving into a pool from a springboard. He landed and splashed a little lava into the air, and then, he was gone.

"What now?" I asked Rachael.

"We wait. I'm not sure how far down the entrance is, but Rob knows to look for a black skull, that signifies the doorway."

So that's what we did, we stood there and waited. I had turned my flashlight off, the smoke at the top of this mountain was too thick for it to make much of a difference. With my eyes still glowing, I scanned the area. No monsters. This was seriously getting creepy.

I looked down into the lava, and even with my enhanced vision, I couldn't see any sign of

Rob. We had no idea what was going on.

"How long can he hold his breath?" I asked Rachael, who had sat down on the edge of the volcano.

"I don't think he needs to. He swam in lava before, just not this deep. I think it works the same way Penny can breathe underwater, just an inherent thing."

I nodded. Demigod powers were extremely weird.

It had been about thirty minutes, and Rob still had not resurfaced. Penny had joined Rachael and me while Blake and Megan were still keeping a lookout.

"Anything yet?" She asked.

"Nothing. I think I need to go in after him." I said.

Penny shook her head.

"If you dive into lava, you'll burn to death. Even with your healing ability."

"I'll make a wind funnel or something around me to keep the lava away. It's been too long." I reasoned.

Before Penny could shoot down my plan, a low rumble starting coming from under our feet. Rachael shot up, pulling her sword from her side and shield from her back. Looking below, I noticed that the smoke was starting to thin, the lava level was lowering at a decent rate. After a few minutes, we saw Rob, standing roughly three hundred feet below us, in front of a black door with a skull engraved in the center. He looked unharmed, maybe a little out of breath, but perfectly fine.

"Sorry, it took so long!" He yelled. "Really had to see through all the lava!"

"You did great!" Rachael yelled back, sheathing her weapons.

Blake and Megan walked up next to us.

"Well, we should get down there," Penny said.

I took the lead, jumping straight down to the ledge Rob was standing. Using the winds, which were much easier to control without the gusts coming from the mountaintop, I broke my fall.

"Just jump!" I screamed to my friends. "I'll catch you!"

They took my advice, and one by one jumped toward the ledge. It was tough, but I managed to get all of them to the door safely.

Penny walked up to the skull on the door and turned the knob. The door instantly swung inward and revealed a staircase that seemed to go on forever. Even with my infrared and night vision, I couldn't see the bottom.

On the door, a timer appeared above the skull, starting at three hours, it began counting down.

"We need to hurry. Once that timer's done, we can't get back unless we all want to swim through lava." Rachael explained.

Penny took the lead, pulling out her sword and shield. I was right behind her, using my flashlight to provide some form of vision to my friends. Once the last person, Megan, had walked through the door, it slammed shut, echoing throughout the staircase.

We walked for a while, descending the stairs. It seemed like forever by the time we saw the bottom. I checked my watch, but the digital numbers were going haywire. First, it said it was one in the morning, the next second, it was three in the afternoon.

"Time gets weird in the Underworld," Rachael said.

"Got it."

We made it to the bottom of the staircase, and in front of us was a wide-open field filled with what looked like ghosts. Transparent people with contorted looks of pain and sadness on their faces.

"The Fields of Asphodel," Penny announced.

The field looked like it went on forever. I couldn't see the end, just millions, maybe even billions, of ghosts. To the left of the Fields of Asphodel, there was a darker sight.

The most prominent feature here was a hill. A man was pushing a boulder to the top. As I watched, the boulder was a few feet away from the peak. Before it reached the top, it fell back to the bottom, the man ran after it.

"Sisyphus?" I asked Rachael.

"Yes. Doomed to forever push that boulder up the hill."

"I'd hate to be that guy," Rob said, walking past me.

Behind the hill, I could make out a glowing valley. Music seemed to be coming from there.

"What's that?" I asked the group.

"Elysium," Blake answered. "Heros go there mainly. It's the best place in the Underworld."

"If they chose to be reborn three times, and reach Elysium all three times, they go to the Fortunate Isles. However, they're not in the Underworld. They're located in the Atlantic Ocean." Rachael elaborated.

"Good to know," I said and then looked around at the area nearest us.

In front of us was a black river. The flow of the river was heading straight to the Fields of Punishment. There was no place for us to cross. Strangely, the water looked like it contained faces. Faces that were in pain.

"The River Styx?" I presumed.

Penny nodded.

"It's a barrier between the mortal world and the Underworld. The faces in the water, are memories of the dead. Goals, dreams, hopes, wishes. It's all that remains."

That just freaked me out even more.

"I take it we have to cross it?"

"Yup," Rob answered.

"The army is probably in some sort of barracks," Blake said. "Best place for that would be in Hades palace." He pointed to our right.

I hadn't noticed it before, but there was a magnificent black stone palace to the right of the Fields of Asphodel. From here, with my eyes still enhanced, I could make out skulls, human skulls, in piles around the doors.

"Guess we should start there," I said.

"We have to be careful. If the Furies catch us, we're as good as dead." Megan added.

"Furies?" I asked.

"Later. We don't have time for any more explanations." Penny ordered.

She walked up to the riverbank, looking at it like it was her worst enemy. She had a look of extreme concentration on her face.

"No good. I can't control it. Jensen, are you able to control the winds down here?"

Focusing, I was able to move the winds, however, it was a whole lot harder down here. I had to concentrate harder than ever, and even then, I was only able to move myself a few inches off the ground.

"Not a whole lot. I think it's because there's less air down here or maybe it's because Hades power is strongest here?"

"Or maybe the Underworld affects our powers." Megan reasoned.

"Either way, Jensen is the only way we can get across the river. Unless we summon Charon, the ferryman. We really don't want to do that, sorta blows our covert op out of the water." Rachael said. "You ready to try?" She addressed me.

I nodded and walked next to Penny.

Summoning a wind current, I was able to get off the ground. I directed myself over the river. When I looked down, I noticed hands trying to grab at me, make an escape, get back to their bodies. I sped up as much as I dared since it was so hard to even keep myself aloft.

Around twenty feet later, I landed on the other side of the river. For once, I was out of breath. This was the first time using my powers actually took something out of me, and I had to do it five more times.

I took a few moments to regroup, get my wits about me. Then, I channeled a wind current to carry Rob over. It went well enough. Since it wasn't me I was trying to support, I was able to put more concentration into it.

Next, I brought over Rachael, then Blake, then Megan. Penny was the last one.

I was pretty exhausted after carrying everyone else over. My mind was going fuzzy, my vision was going in and out. Black dots were popping around everything I saw. My eyes closed. That's when it went wrong.

Penny's scream is what brought me back to reality. My eyes shot open. Penny was falling in the River Styx. I ran as fast as I could. She was inches away from the water.

Putting all of the strength I could into my legs, I jumped. I wrapped my arms around Penny's waist. A few moments later, we crashed into the opposite shore. I skid across the black rocks, my arms tearing open, blood flowing all around me. Penny was at my side in seconds.

The cuts on my arm were healing, but from the effort of controlling the winds, and jumping to save Penny, I was starting to blackout. She forced my mouth open and placed some ambrosia on my tongue. I chewed it as best I could, and instantly, my body felt reinvigorated. I sat up and looked at Penny.

"Good catch." She said, smiling.

"Thanks."

Penny stood up and extended her hand. I took it and she helped me up. Looking back across the river, our friends stood there, looks of relief on their faces.

"How are we gonna get across?" Penny asked.

"Well, now that I'm back with it slightly, I should be able to jump us across."

Penny put her arms around my neck and locked in a vice grip. I picked her legs up around my waist and ran toward the river bank. At the edge, I jumped and easily cleared the twenty feet gap.

When we landed, Penny slid from around me.

"Let's get going, we took way too much time here." She ordered and starting walking towards Hades' palace.

11

Chapter Eleven: The army of Hades

We made our way to the palace, following the river bank. Even being in the Underworld, we didn't see any monsters, not even the Furies.

Hades palace was roughly a mile away from where we entered. It was short enough of a walk, but with all of the ghosts floating around us, it made it seem like forever. The spirits seemed to be sapping our will to live. After only about ten minutes of walking, I felt like giving up hope. However, whenever I looked at Penny or Rachael, my spirits lifted, reminding me that we were here to do a job.

I looked back over at the River Styx. The faces that swirled in the water seemed to be following us with their eyes. Every now and then a hand would reach out towards me, wanting to drag me in. Whenever this happened, I moved a little to my left, avoiding the water.

Once we got close to the palace, I would say about three hundred feet away, Penny had us stop. She made us take cover behind a large boulder.

"The only way in, that I saw anyway, is the front doors. That's obviously not going to work. It would throw our plan out the window. Jensen, can you hear anything?"

I adjusted my hearing, trying to catch any signs of a monster.

"Inside, I hear a lot of growling, snarling, and hissing. It's all on one floor. About a mile past the entrance. It's echoing. Like they're outside."

Penny and Rachael looked at each other, thinking.

"So, there's an open area, big enough to hold all of the monsters in the Underworld," Penny said.

"Likely, there's room for more as they come out of Tartarus," Rachael added.

"Rob, is there anything you can do to get us in there?" Penny asked.

Rob took his bag off of his shoulder and started looking through it. He was pulling random things out and was handing them to me; gears, wires, wrenches. Finally, he found what he was looking for.

It was something that looked like a miniature t-shirt cannon that you would see at a baseball game. However, instead of a shirt inside the barrel, there was a grappling hook.

"Bronze rope should hold us." He said, smiling. "It's got about two hundred feet in it. More than enough."

How the little gun could hold two hundred feet of bronze rope, I had no idea, but I trusted Rob.

"Good. Get close, and set it up" Penny ordered Rob. "Blake, cover him."

Blake and Rob nodded and moved out from our hiding spot. Blake had his shield and sword out, walking backward in a crouched position, protecting Rob from behind. When they were ten feet from the front wall, Rob took aim.

The cannon made almost no noise when it was fired, but the grappling hook flew through the air. It latched on to the roof, it's steel prongs poking through the stone. Rob tugged on it a few times to make sure it was secure, then motioned to us that it was good to go.

Penny, Rachael, Megan and I crouched and ran towards him.

"From now on, use hand signals. If you need to talk, whisper. Jensen will be able to hear you and convey the message to me."

Everyone nodded.

Blake was the first one to climb the rope. He climbed like he had been doing it his whole life, which he might of. When he reached the top, Rachael went up. Then Rob, Megan, and Penny. I stayed at the bottom for a few seconds, making sure there were no threats behind us.

Once I was confident we were in the clear, I leaped to the top of the wall, leaving the rope where it was. The wall was only a sixty feet tall, so it wasn't too hard to land on the top. When I joined my friends, Rob made to remove the grappling hook.

Blake stopped him, shaking his head. I knew what he was thinking. If we needed to make a quick escape, this was our best way out. He pulled the rope up and coiled it on the roof, just in case.

In front of us, we could see all of Hades' palace. It looked endless. The entire roof was made out of the same black volcanic rock I had seen earlier. I bent down, extended the claw on my index finger, and tried to poke a hole in it. Nothing. This stone was the hardest thing I've ever come across. My claws could cut through almost anything. Obviously, the wall wasn't made of the same stuff, but the roof was extremely sturdy.

Penny motioned for us to continue forward, and we did just that. In a crouching run, we went as fast as we could. Now that we were out of the Fields of Asphodel, it didn't seem to take very long to clear a mile. I knew how far we had gone when Rob, who was slightly ahead of us, almost fell into a giant hole. I caught up just in time to grab the back of his shirt.

Pulling him back, I looked down into the hole of the roof.

Below us was a sea of monsters, all separated by fences. From what I could tell, they were parted into sections of the type of monster they were. All of the hellhounds and there were a lot of them, were together. I saw groups of mormo spirits, several dozens. There were giants, griffins, huge spiders at least the size of minivans, and a bunch of other monsters I haven't seen or heard of. Right below us was a fenced-off area, larger than the others, filled with, and I couldn't believe it, dragons.

"Dragons?" I whispered to Penny.

She nodded.

"They're going to the hardest to kill. We might have to do that by hand. I hope to avoid that." She answered.

The dragons looked exactly as you'd expect. Each one was at least fifteen feet long, giant teeth that looked like they could rip apart an armored car, just like their claws. Their tails were covered with sharp barbs and their wings. Their wings were at least as long as their bodies. They ranged in color from dark black, to pale white, and everything in between. The scales on their

110

bodies looked like plate metal.

I looked around the edge of the hole and saw a little ledge that we could walk on.

I tapped Penny on the shoulder and pointed to what I saw. She nodded.

"Sneak." She whispered. "We can't be seen. We'll start at the back, and make our way forward. Go in groups of two until all of the charges are placed."

Rob opened his bag again and handed us all a handful of small packets that had microchips on the outside. They seemed to contain tiny amounts of liquid.

"Greek fire charges. If you place it on the fence, it should explode and take out the entire pen. The dragons might need three of four. Actually, any leftover you have, put them there. We need firepower." He explained in a hushed voice.

Once we had all of our explosives secure in our bags, I led the way around the edge.

It was dark up here, which was good. I took the lead to make sure we didn't trip. Slowly but surely, we made it to the other side of the hole, which was about a mile and a half from where we started.

At the back of the clearing, there were roughly a dozen empty pens. I jumped down first and caught all of my friends as they joined me. We crouched down again and split into teams. Blake and Megan, Rachael and Rob, and Penny and I.

Most of the monsters were distracted and paid us no attention. Penny and I started on the right side of the clearing. All we had to do is place the packet of Greek fire on the fence, and it instantly sealed itself to the wood. Everything seemed to be going according to plan. Nothing noticed us.

Penny and I had made it about halfway through our side of pens when everything went wrong.

Megan and Blake were almost done on the back left, setting the last of their charges. Rob and Rachael were almost done as well. The only pen they had left was the dragons. Rob walked up to it, and place a few charges on the closest post. He seemed to have dropped one on the ground from what I could see. When he bent over to pick it up, he smacked his head on the fence post. The sound resonated through the clearing.

Penny and I hit the ground in a prone position. I noticed Blake and Megan did the same. Rachael was grabbing Rob by the back of his shirt, but it was too late.

The dragons had turned around, at least twenty of them, all staring at Rob. He stood there, in a stunned trance, looking at the dragons. The one closest to Rob opened its mouth and let out a terrible roar that made the fence posts and walls all around the clearing, shake. All of the other monsters were now looking at the dragon pin, directly at Rob and Rachael.

Without thinking, I jumped into action.

I pulled my flashlight from my pocket and turned it into a spear. With all my strength I threw it at the dragon closest to my friends. Surprisingly, the point of my spear entered its neck, and the dragon burst into flames with a look of confusion on its face.

In the pin next to me, several large spiders looked at me. I shifted right in front of them, and sliced the spiders closest to me with my claws, turning them to flames. Jumping out from behind the pen, I ran towards the dragons enclosure. All of their attention was on me now. Rachael and Rob were backing up.

Before I could engage in battle, a loud boom echoed through the area. I stopped dead in my tracks and turned to the origin of the noise.

Standing in a doorway, that had just been thrown open, stood the man I saw in my dream.

Six feet tall, black robes flowing around him. His black fire beard and eyes blazed, but not out of anger. It was hard to place the emotion, but I think it was joy.

"Son. Of. Zeus." Hades said, mockingly clapping his hands. "I was hoping you would join us."

Hades waved his hand. My friends were pulled from their hiding spots as if an invisible rope was attached around their waists. They stopped next to me.

"I was thinking of killing you when I destroyed your school," Hades said as he stepped into the clearing towards us. "But since you decided to enter my domain, it seems only right I dispose of you here."

Hades clapped his hands again. From the doorway he had just walked, three women flew out on black leathery wings.

"The Furies," Megan whispered, fear in her voice.

The Furies looked like regular women, except their razor-sharp talons where their toes and fingers should be, their wings, and fangs. Each one of the creatures also had a whip attached to their side.

"Take these, demigods," he said the word with disgust, "to the throne room. I have some questions for them before their demise."

The Furies took their whips from their waists and flicked them through the air, wrapping my friends and me into a group. We were shoulder to shoulder, and the Furies lifted us into the air.

The pulled us through the doorway and down a long black hallway. While we went, I

shifted again, back into human form. I remembered my spear, and how I had left it lying on the ground in the dragon pen.

When we reached the end of the hallway, the Furies flew into a set of solid black stone doors.

Hades' throne room was immaculate, in a dark, deathly, type of way. The walls were pure black, like everything else in the palace. Hades' throne sat on top of a mound of assorted metals. I noticed gold, bronze, and iron. His throne itself looked like it was carved out of human bone, with a red cushion on the seat.

The walls of the room were covered in torches that burned with black fire, which surprisingly covered the room in dim light. There were two doors on either side of Hades' throne, each guarded by what seemed to be civil war soldiers that carried muskets.

The Furies thew us down in front of the throne, a little harder than was required. We sat there, still bound by their whips. A few moments later, Hades materialized in a flash of black flame.

He was sitting on his throne, and in his hand, he held a bronze spear.

"A very nice weapon, Jensen Smith," Hades said, running his finger down my spear.

"Godly bronze. Nearly indestructible. Did you know that?"

I didn't say anything. True, I didn't know that godly bronze was a thing. I just thought that my weapon had special properties since it was made by Rob's dad. However, I wasn't going to admit that. I was too busy trying to think a way out of this.

"You see, Jensen. My brother is a very powerful being. He sets our laws and rules. All gods must abide by them, even me." Hades stabbed my spear into the floor. "However, he chose to break one of these laws. He had you. You, the abomination." He said the last word like I was the worst thing imaginable.

"My father doesn't define me," I said, spite in my voice. "You have no idea who I am."

Hades laughed.

"Who you are, or how you act currently does not matter. At some point, like all of your kind, you will commit atrocities. You must die."

"Why haven't you killed me yet then?" I had no idea why he was waiting.

"You see, son of Zeus, I have a few questions for you."

"I'm not going to answer any questions."

"We'll see," Hades said. "First question, why are you here? Obviously, it was due to my army, but what is your plan?"

I stayed quiet. My friends didn't speak up either. We were on the same page. Hades didn't know about the charges, we still had a chance.

"Nothing? I will find out eventually. One way or the other."

Again, we said nothing.

"Second, how prepared is your school for my attack? I wish to run into as little resistance as possible."

"More than prepared." Penny offered. I looked at her, and she looked angry. "You don't stand a chance."

Hades laughed, and the throne room shook. I just noticed how much power was radiating off of him. It felt like I was standing right in front of a raging forest fire.

"Unlikely, daughter of Poseidon." He continued with his questioning. "Finally, will you be receiving assistance from the other gods?"

This time, even Penny stayed quiet. Honestly, we didn't know if the other gods were going to help us. I was hoping that they would, but we haven't heard anything due to not being at school.

"Still nothing? That's fine." Hades clapped his hands again. The Furies whips untied from around us.

Before we could even react, the Furies lassoed our bags and weapons, yanking them off of us.

"Take them below. Leave the sea princess behind."

The whips secured themselves around us again, except for Penny who was being held by one Fury. The other two pulled my friends and me back behind the throne room to the door on the right. It was pushed open by the civil war soldiers. When they were up close, they looked like decaying skeletons but had full movement.

The Furies dragged us down a staircase, not bothering to lift us up, so we hit every step on the way down. Once at the bottom, they took us far into the back. We passed what seemed to be jail cells. Most were empty, but a few had occupants. Humans, from what I could tell, looked to be hundreds of years old.

We reached the last cell, big enough to hold at least ten people. One of the Furies unclipped keys from her side and opened the door. They threw us inside with a snap of their whips and we hit the ground hard.

I got up as quick as I could, but before I could make a run for it, the jail cell door slammed shut. I ran directly into it. We were trapped.

"What are we going to do?" Rob asked Rachael. "He's got Penny up there."

"I don't know Rob, let me think." Rachael had tears in her eyes, but a look of pure concentration on her face.

"How were you going to detonate the charges?" I asked Rob.

He tapped his watch.

"I configured one of the buttons to set them off. If I do it now though, it'll probably kill

us."

"Okay. There goes that plan."

I sat down on the floor against the wall. Hades hadn't taken any of our watches, which means I still had my shield. However, my friends didn't have anything to fight with. After a few minutes of sitting, I got up and walked over to the bars of the cell.

They looked like the same type of stone that the roof of the palace was made of. I extended my claws and took a swipe. No luck. I tried pushing on them, putting all my strength into. Ten tons of pressure and the cell door didn't even budge.

"That's not possible." I murmured.

I went into a full shift. Maybe the extra strength will do something. If the door was able to take thirty tons of force, it was able to take anything.

I pushed. The bars shook slightly but didn't do more than that. Kicking the door out of anger, I shifted back to human and sat back down.

"I take it that didn't work?" Megan asked me.

"Not even a little. I was putting all my strength into that. A rock can't be that strong."

"It's underworld obsidian," Blake said. "It's the strongest material in the world. Great for weapons, it can kill anything. Hades' own blade is made out of the stuff. It can even keep gods out of commission for decades."

"Also, it can only be forged in lava that has been enhanced by a god. The best god is Hephaestus, but any god can do it." Rob added. "If it's not my dad's work it's weaker, but still the strongest weapons are created by the stuff. However, they normally have a crack in them. A weak point."

"Unless they're made by Hephaestus. Almost none of them are though. We only have one at school made by him, and we only take it out in the worst of circumstances. As I said, it's wickedly powerful. It can entrap the soul of the person it hits." Blake explained.

"Wow." That's all I could say.

Before anyone else could speak, one of the Furies flew by. I noticed the whip and keys dangling at her side. If only I could get the keys.

We were stuck in here with no way out, and we were running out of time. Rachael said that time got weird in the Underworld. I had no idea if we've been down here for an hour or only fifteen minutes. I was hoping we had enough time left. I pictured the countdown clock at the top of the staircase, counting down to one. If that happened, we'd be trapped here forever.

I sat thinking, watching the Fury fly back down the hallway. Then I heard it. A blood-curdling scream coming from upstairs.

Instantly, I shot to my feet, running to the cell door. My friends were at my side.

"No. He can't be torturing her." Rachael said, fresh tears in her eyes.

Anger started flowing through me, more fierce than I have ever felt before.

"He's not going to be doing it for long. I have a plan."

12

Chapter Twelve: Rescues and explosions

We waited a while longer, keeping track of the Furies. Every five minutes one of them did a pass. All of them had a set of keys.

The whole time we waited, my rage stayed in the red. My vision had actually started to become weird, everything sort of had a blue/red hue to it.

After the third pass of one of the Furies, I couldn't wait anymore.

Focusing as hard as I could, I managed to have a light wind current loop around the keys on the Furies waist. She didn't notice, thankfully. I urged the keys to float to me and grabbed them.

As they landed in my hand, I heard Penny scream again. I went into overdrive.

Handing the keys to Rob, he quickly found the correct key, put it in the lock, and opened the door.

I took my shield watch off of my wrist and handed it to Blake as we planned. Then, without waiting for the others, I shifted and took off.

The Fury that had just passed our cell turned around at the last second. She went for her whip, but I was too quick. Just as her fingers were closing around her weapon, I slashed my claws across her throat. She didn't go down immediately, so I sank my teeth into her neck. That did it. The monster burst into black flames and was no more.

I ran up the steps at full speed. There were at least three hundred of them, but I hardly noticed. When I reached the top, I kicked the door open, and it flew off its hinges and across the throne room. The civil war guards moved back and aimed their guns at me. They went off, and I felt bullets enter my stomach.

They exited out the back. I grabbed the soldier's guns and snapped them in half. Each of the soldiers pulled knives and charged me, but they lasted a whole two seconds. I cut them down with one swipe of my claws, and they crumbled to dust.

I walked into the throne room and saw a terrible scene.

Penny lay on the ground, deep cuts across her face and arms. A small pool of blood was on the floor under her. Hades was standing above her, my spear in his hand. He apparently had spun around when I kicked the door in. When he looked at me, he smiled.

"Jensen. Nice of you to join us."

"Move away from her," I said, a growl in my voice. My rage seemed to be taking over.

"No, I don't think I will." He raised my spear in the air.

Before he could do anything else, I picked up his throne. Easily three tons. I threw it straight at the god. He was caught off guard. When the chair hit him, he flew fifty feet across the room, dropping my spear where he stood.

My friends joined me a second later. When they saw Penny, they all gasped.

"Get her out of here. Get your stuff, and go. Hades is mine." I ordered.

"No! We can't leave you to fight a god on your own." Rachael argued.

I turned and looked at her. She looked me square in the eyes, terrified.

"He's going to kill all of our friends. He hurt Penny. He wants to kill me. I'm not going to let him do any of that. Now go."

No one else argued.

When I turned back, Hades was getting to his feet. He had a cut on his head, silver blood dripping from it.

"You're dead, son of Zeus!" Hades yelled.

He pulled a long black sword from the inside of his robes, the same one I saw in my dream.

I ran forward as fast as I could, straight at the god. My friends were right behind me, but considerably slower. When I passed Penny, I scooped my spear from the ground. Quickly, I changed it into a sword.

Hades was quick.

When I was six feet away from him he swung his sword. I parried his strike and made one of my own. Hades seemed to become transparent. My blade past right through him, causing no damage. He summoned a ball of black fire in his free hand and thrust it into my chest. I flew back at least ten feet.

I stood up quickly and saw my shirt was on fire. I ripped it off.

"You cannot defeat me, nephew." Hades chuckled.

"You are not my family!" I yelled defiantly and charged again.

Hades swung his sword again, this time, I changed my sword into a shield and blocked it. With my claws, I swiped at his sword arm. This time I made contact. More silver blood gushed from the wound.

Hades recoiled, holding his arm.

"How dare you spill ichor! You are not worthy!" Hades seemed extremely angry, but I didn't care.

I stayed on the offensive. Transforming my shield back into a spear, I struck Hades in the chest, this time, he didn't become transparent. My spear tip caught him right under the ribs. While it was lodged there, I summoned as much electricity from my body as possible and surged it into the god's body. He went flying.

Taking a chance, I looked back at my friends. They had retrieved their belongings and were getting Penny to her feet. She looked awful, pale. Megan was attempting to patch some of her wounds while they were lifting her up.

"GO!" I yelled at them. "I'll follow. Just get out of here!"

They took my advice. Blake slid my watch off his wrist and threw it to me. I picked it out of the air and put it on. Then, Blake picked Penny up, placed her on his back, and ran out of the throne room.

I spun back around, just as Hades was getting to his feet. The front of his robes was still smoking, but he looked unharmed.

"You're dead." He sounded calm.

In the blink of an eye, Hades was in front of me. I didn't even see him move. He wrapped his hand around my throat and lifted me off the ground.

"You are not meant for this world. Once you die, I will destroy your friends.

Then, your pack."

That was it, he crossed the line.

I kicked the god in the chest with both of my legs. Hades flew back a few feet but managed to stay standing. Before he could move, I ran at him, spear in hand. I jammed it into his chest, the point sticking out of his back. I moved in close, right next to his godly ear.

"If I ever see you again, I'll wipe you from existence," I whispered in his ear.

I channeled yet another strike of lightning through my spear.

When I pulled my weapon free, Hades dropped to his knees. Silver blood gushed from the wound I had just made. He looked up to me.

"You will burn."

With those words, the god burst into black flames. The force of the blast threw me off my feet and sent me sailing across the room. I crashed into the pile of metal that previously contained the throne.

My chest was engulfed in the black fire, my skin burning off. I patted my chest and extinguished the flames. The burns on my body started to heal, but slowly.

I got to my feet and look around. The throne room was burning to the ground. I needed to get out.

Running as fast as I could, I made my way to the doors. I burst through and looked around for the exit. It was on the far end of the corridor. I started running as more fire blasted out of the throne room, scorching my hair and my pant legs.

I hit top speed and crashed through the entrance doors. Slipping on a skull, I rolled down the few steps that were there. When I got up, I saw my friends about half a mile away, running through the Fields of Asphodel. I started running again, catching up to them easily.

"Rob!" I said and startled him. "Blow it."

Immediately, Rob slapped the button on his watch. Behind us, green flames erupted from the palace mingling with the black. I could hear distance wails of dying monsters.

"Let's go!" I ordered.

We kept a good pace the last half mile to the entrance. I was still shifted.

When we got to the river bank, I picked up my friends one by one and jumped across the water. Once everyone was across, we ran up the staircase.

I took the burden of carrying Penny from Blake so we could keep at our top speed.

When we were a hundred feet from the top, I could see the timer ticking down. We only had two minutes left.

Once we reached the top, Rob opened his bag and pulled out another grappling hook cannon. He shot it at the mouth of the volcano and anchored it to the door. Blake went first, followed by Rachael, and Megan. Using a wind current, I lifted Penny to the top, where Blake grabbed her.

Once Penny was safe, I heard a roar from behind me. Rob and I spun around.

Flying up the stairs were the dragons from Hades' army. The lead dragon was only a few hundred feet away.

"Rob, go! I'll hold them off." I ordered.

"No!"

"I said go!" And picked him up, and threw him at the rope.

He grabbed on and began to climb to the top. I looked over at the timer. I had less than thirty seconds. The ground started to rumble, and I looked down. Lava began to rise. However, I couldn't worry about that now.

The dragons were now on top of me. I controlled the winds and flew backward off of the ledge. Fire was being directed at me now by the dragon in the lead. Now that I was above ground, I had better control over the winds. I forced a wind current into the jet of flame and extinguished it. However, I was still in danger.

The dragons were fast. One of them caught up to me and sank its fangs into my left arm. I stabbed at it with my claws, and thankfully, I punctured its skin. It burst into flames. My arm wasn't healing quite yet.

Then I noticed the other dragons coming up close. I glanced at the door, and the timer was at zero. The lava was now climbing faster. I urged the winds to carry me up as fast as possible, and the dragons follow. My friends had made it to the bottom of the volcano funnel. Megan was loading an arrow, and firing at the dragons.

I raised my spear in the air, an idea forming. Concentrating as hard as I could, I summoned a lightning bolt from the sky, but not just any old regular bolt. I kept a solid stream of lightning channeling into my spear, keeping it held at the point for as long as possible. At the same time, I channeled all of my internal electricity to the same point on my spear. The effort was almost too much. My vision became blurry, my other senses dulled. I vaguely heard yelling from below me. My control over the wind was failing. In the last effort, I aimed my spear towards the lava.

Next, I just remember the heat and burns all over my body. I also remember slamming into the ground, and water hitting my face. After that, I remember nothing.

I woke up hours later, water was still hitting my face. Opening my eyes, I looked around, still no strength to lift my head. From what I could see, I was lying near a river. Trees sat along the bank. Huge rocks were breaking up the flow of water.

A few moments later, I heard someone's voice.

"I found him! Bring Penny, he's in a river!"

It was Rachael.

I felt her hands on my shoulders as she flipped me on to my back. I was on the bank of the river, the water I was feeling on my face was being splashed as it hit the rocks. Rachael pulled her bag off her shoulders and pulled out some ambrosia. She put a piece in my mouth, and I chewed it as best as I could. The chocolate cake with strawberry icing taste. It was amazing.

My body still felt broken, but I was able to raise my head and look at Rachael properly. From over her shoulder, I saw Blake and Rob carrying Penny. Megan was walking next to them and going through her medical bag.

Blake and Rob placed Penny in the water. She still looked terrible, her wounds were still bleeding, and she looked pale. Once her body touched the water, however, color rushed to her face. Her wounds started to heal almost as quickly as mine normally do. Her eyes snapped open and she gasped. After a minute or two, Penny was able to stand up and looked like nothing happened.

"Thanks, guys. I didn't think I was going to make it out of there." She told my friends, then she saw me. "Oh, my gods." She whispered and knelt next to me.

"I'm okay," I said weakly.

My wounds started healing a little quicker now thanks to the ambrosia. I could sense I had broken all of my ribs again, my right leg, and my left arm. Also, there was a crack in my skull. At least being a werewolf helped me identify injuries.

Penny grabbed my hand looking at Megan.

"Can you fix him?" She asked.

Megan crouched down next to me and held her hands over my chest. She started chanting in what I thought was ancient Greek. It was some sort of prayer. Her hands started glowing gold. She stopped after about a minute, and to be honest, I was starting to feel a lot better.

"I said a prayer to my father," Megan explained. "Now, it's up to Jensen's werewolf physiology and my dad. I think he'll be okay though."

Penny gripped my hand even tighter, and I saw Rachael scrunch her eyebrows. I didn't think that this was the time for her to be jealous.

I was able to prop myself up on my elbows. Everyone seemed to be unharmed.

"What happened?" I asked.

Penny was the one to answer.

"When you shot lightning into the volcano, it erupted. I was with it enough to tell that."

"Once the lava shot out of the volcano, you were gone. I saw your body fly for what seemed like forever." Rob added.

"We only made it out because of Rob. He used his body and his shield to block the eruption from hitting us. Then we went and looked for you, and found you here. About three miles away from the mountain." Rachael finished the story.

I sat there processing the information for a minute. How I was alive, I had no idea. I shouldn't have survived a volcanic eruption or the fall I took. When I looked around, I could see ash and smoke rising into the air in the distance.

"What are we going to do now?" I asked the group.

It was a few moments until anyone answered.

"Once you're able to walk, we need to head to the Pacific. When we get there, I can ask my dad for help." Penny said, a look of pain on her face.

I knew she didn't like getting help from her dad, her response at the beginning of the quest when Rachael suggested it told me that.

Rob and Blake helped me up and led me over to sit with my back to a tree. Once I was situated, Rob took food out of his bag, made a fire, and started cooking. While I was waiting to eat, the cuts and burns all over my body healed over. My leg was almost mended, as were my ribs and arm. The crack in my skull hadn't even started healing yet, but I knew it was a matter of time. Once the rest of my body was restored, my body would focus on my head, and heal it quickly. This wasn't the first cracked skull I had.

Rob finished cooking the venison steaks and handed them out. I ate mine in about ten seconds flat. I hadn't realized how hungry I was. After devouring my food, I looked around.

By the river, there wasn't much besides rocks and trees. I could smell the ash in the distance, and noticed that it had started falling near us.

"We need to get going soon," I said.

"You're in no shape." Penny pointed out.

True, I wasn't in the best shape, but after sitting here and eating, I was starting to heal faster. I could at least walk. I shared this with Penny. She looked up into the sky, at the ash that was starting to fall like light snow.

"Pack up. We need to head to the ocean. From there, I'll talk to my dad. He'll get us home. I hope."

No one questioned what she meant, but I don't understand why her father wouldn't help her.

Once everyone had finished eating, they packed everything up, and Blake helped me to my feet. My ribs and leg still felt weak, but I was able to walk, even if it was with a limp.

We made our way through the forest and across the rivers. Penny was able to slow the currents down so we could pass. It was going slow for a while since my friends were busy making sure I didn't fall over. However, about an hour into our journey, my leg and ribs were fully healed.

Rachael was walking next to me to make sure I didn't fall.

"That was probably the hardest fight I've ever had," I told her.

"Well, he is one of the three major gods. I would assume that it wouldn't have been a walk in the park."

I laughed.

"No kidding. What was really weird, he bled silver. Like Damysus."

I hadn't made note of it before, but I did find it strange that the giant had silver blood.

"Ichor, the blood of immortals. Gods can't die, but they can bleed." Rachael said.

"How long does it normally take them to recover from major injuries?" I asked.

"Depends. Why?"

I told Rachael of the encounter with Hades, everything that happened after my friends left.

Rachael stared at me for a few moments.

"From something like that, it might take him a few weeks to recover."

"What about the monsters?"

"Well, some of the stronger one, like the dragons, it will take them longer to reform. However, once Hades is back to full strength, he can probably raise the others quickly; hellhounds, mormo and the like. I give it maybe six weeks until Hades is ready to attack again."

I pondered that for a few moments. After all of the damage I did to Hades, and almost all of his monsters were destroyed, we only bought ourselves six weeks, at most. Hopefully, the gods can decide if they are going to help us by then.

We walked a little while longer before I felt one hundred percent. I checked my watch, and it was after six in the afternoon now. It seemed like it was a week ago that we were starting our trek up the mountain.

It only took us another hour to reach the ocean. We walked to a deserted area of a beach. I couldn't see anyone within a mile of our location. Penny walked to the edge of the water, waves crashing at her feet. Looking out over the sea, I saw fish jumping from the water.

"You all need to wait here." Penny addressed us, looking out across the water.

"I didn't think we had a choice," Rob said sarcastically. Megan elbowed him in the ribs.

Penny continued as if Rob hadn't spoken.

"If I'm not back in an hour, find another way home. Don't come after me."

"Why wouldn't you come back?" I asked, confused.

Penny didn't answer, I looked at Rachael.

"I'll explain later." She whispered.

Penny took her bag off of her shoulder and set it on the ground. Then, she started walking into the waves. After a few moments, her head sank below the water as she dove into the depths of the ocean.

We sat on the beach, Rachael next to me making sure I was okay. Megan had pulled a blanket out of her bag for us to sit on. Blake pulled some beef jerky from his bag for us to snack on. It seemed like forever while we waited for Penny.

After about half an hour, I finally dug into what I was thinking about.

"So, why wouldn't Penny come back? Isn't she going to see her dad?" I addressed Rachael.

She sighed.

"It's not even her dad that worries her. It's his wife."

"Amphitrite? Is that right?" I asked, remembering the myth.

Rachael nodded.

"Daughter of Nereus, who was the eldest son of Pontus."

"Pontus? Who's that?"

"He was the first god of the sea, before the Olympians, before even Oceanus, who is the actual manifestation of the ocean."

Godly family trees were confusing.

"Okay, so Poseidon's wife is the daughter of a guy who is the son of a sea god who was the god of the sea before the sea existed?"

"Kind of, it's more like, Pontus was the original manifestation of the sea, before Oceanus. After Oceanus came around, Pontus more or less just dissolved."

"Okay, anyway, what about Penny? Why is she worried?" I pressed on, after the short history lesson.

"Right. Anyway, Amphitrite is always jealous whenever her husband has other children. Whether they be cyclopes, nymphs, or demigods. It's worse with demigods though, she absolutely hates Poseidon's mortal children." Rachael explained.

"Okay. Why would that matter to Penny though? Who cares if her stepmom hates her?"

"Penny has met her father before, actually lived with him for a few months. Towards the end of her stay there, Amphitrite tried to kill her. She hasn't been back since."

I was speechless. Penny's godly stepmother tried to kill her. She went back into the ocean to ask her father for help.

"What did Poseidon do? When he found out about that, I mean." I asked after a minute or two of silence.

"From what Penny told me, he got angry. Really angry. He caused the tsunami in Japan in twenty-eleven."

"Wow." That's all I could say.

"Yeah. Then Penny came back to school."

I wanted to ask more questions, but I didn't get a chance. Just as I opened my mouth to speak, the ocean started to churn. The water started to froth and spin. A geyser erupted fifty feet from the shore.

Through the haze of the water, I could see a man standing behind a girl. He stood roughly three feet taller than her. In his hand, I could see what looked like a trident.

The geyser moved forward. Before it touched the sand, the water splashed down into the ocean and the waves retreated. Standing in front of us was Penny, and a man with short brown hair, a Greek tunic, and sea-green eyes. The same man I saw in the painting in Zeus' temple; Poseidon.

13

Chapter Thirteen: Our deep-sea adventure

Poseidon and Penny walked towards us. Poseidon was smiling, but Penny looked sad. I gave her a quizzical look, but she just shook her head and mouthed: later. I didn't speak up, but I was a little concerned.

When they reached us, everyone got to their knees and knelt. I decided it best to follow their lead.

"Hello, demigods," Poseidon said, with a deep booming voice.

"Guys, this is my dad." Penny offered.

"Hello. No need to kneel." Poseidon was still smiling.

We stood.

"Dad, this is; Rachael, Rob, Blake, Megan, and Jensen"

When Penny said my name and pointed at me, her father narrowed his eyes.

"Yes, Jensen Smith. My brother's son. How are you?" He extended his hand to me. I took it and shook.

"All things considered, I've been worse," I responded.

Poseidon started smiling again.

"I hold no ill will Jensen. My brother has many flaws and has made many mistakes. From what my daughter has told me about you, you are not one of them. I'm truly happy you are traveling with Penelope."

I didn't know what to say. Thankfully, Rob spoke up.

"Lord Poseidon, it's a pleasure to meet you. I had a few inventions I wanted to run by you."

Rob reached into his bag and started bringing out blueprints.

"I would be happy to see them, son of Hephaestus. However, first, I think we should have a meal, and get you a ride home."

Poseidon waved his trident over our heads in a wide arc. Little particles that sort of looked like salt rained down. I felt a shiver go through my spine, but after a few moments, it was gone.

"You can breathe underwater, and you'll be able to see just fine. The effects will last a few hours. Follow me." Poseidon turned and walked back towards the water.

"Trust me," Penny whispered to us before following.

We picked up our belongings and jogged to meet Penny's dad. Penny parted the water as we approached, which earned her an impressive look from her father. The water was only parted for about twenty feet. Once we submerged, I took a deep breath, expecting my lungs to fill with water. However, I was breathing regular air.

There seemed to be some sort of protective bubble around me that constantly produced new air. If I focused, I could even control it. The air stretched about an inch around my body, and I could circulate it.

We walked about a mile underwater, until Poseidon stopped us. He led us to a chariot. It was bright green and seemed to glow with a bronze haze. In the front, instead of horses, there were two giant sailfish. Blue in color, with magnificent fins that stretched along their backs. They seemed to be at least the size of hammerhead sharks.

"Fastest fish in the ocean. When blessed by my father, they're even faster. They can break the sound barrier underwater." Penny explained.

"Please, climb in." Poseidon offered, stepping into the back of the chariot.

We accepted his offer and climbed in behind the sea god. Poseidon grabbed the reins of the chariot and flicked them. Instantly, the sailfish flexed their fins and took off.

I was flung back so hard that I almost fell out of the chariot. I had to use my claws to stay attached to our ride. Everyone else, besides Penny, seemed to be unseated too. Rachael flew back into me, and Rob, Blake, and Megan were holding on for dear life. Using my strength, I pulled Rachael and myself back into a standing position.

We traveled on the seafloor. To our left, a school of fish swam by. On our right, a dolphin was trying to catch up to us, but to no avail. Speeding through the ocean depths felt like a dream. I never imagined doing anything like this.

Just as I was starting to enjoy myself, Poseidon pulled up on the reins and the sailfish pulled the chariot off of the ground. In the distance, there was a magnificent green palace, the same color as the chariot. The entire building gave off the same bronze glow as well. We raced toward the castle with blinding speed.

Poseidon guided the chariot over a thirty feet high wall and landed it in front of some stables. We all stepped off and I looked around.

The stables held different types of fish and monsters. Sailfish and whale sharks floated in their pins. Fish horses were present among the creatures as well. The front of the monsters were horses, with strong fishtails coming out of the back. They were a beautiful blue color and almost blended in with water. There were about ten of them in the stables.

"Hippocampi. Sea-horses." Penny said, walking up behind me.

"They're beautiful." I turned and looked at her.

"Yeah." She laughed. "Let's go." She turned and walked towards her father, who was walking to the palace.

Penny's dad led us into an entranceway. The hallway looked normal enough, the same color as the outside. It was more or less plain; no pictures on the walls, no underwater fires.

We followed the sea god down the hallway. When we reached the end, he pushed open a gigantic set of coral doors and lead us into a dining area. There was a table that was twenty feet long in the middle of the room. The table itself was made of seashells, glittering white in the light being projected from greek fire lamps that were hung along the walls. Chairs made of coral lined the table. Poseidon took a seat at the head of the table.

"Please, sit." He offered, waving his hand.

A second later six chairs moved back from the table. Penny walked up and took the seat to the right of her father. I sat next to her, and Rachael next to me. The rest of our friends filled the chairs on the opposite side of the table.

Once everyone was seated, Poseidon clapped his hands. A few moments later, platters of food were coming from a door in the back of the room. Piles of vegetables and fruit landed on the table, apparently being carried on the water currents. Looking around the table, I noticed there was no meat. Penny saw me looking.

"No meat here. We can't bring down any land animals to cook, and my father refuses to eat fish." She whispered.

I nodded and reached for the plate of mangos.

"So, demigods." Poseidon started saying. "Penny told me about your journey so far. However," he turned towards me. "I would like to know the details of your battle with Hades."

I explained to him everything that happened while I fought the god of the Underworld. While I was talking, Poseidon looked at me with interest, his fingers interlocked in front of his mouth, his hair flowing around him with the water current.

When I was done, the sea god waited a few moments before saying anything.

"That's very impressive. However, it's not surprising that my brother's strongest child was able to go toe to toe with his uncle."

"Who says I'm the strongest?" I inquired.

Poseidon laughed.

"My boy, you are the strongest son of Zeus since Heracles. There is no contest. Hades is terrified of you."

"My husband is correct." Said a voice from the back of the room.

From the door, the food had come, walked a woman, maybe a foot shorter than Poseidon. The woman was beautiful. She had long red hair that was braided down the back. Her sea-green eyes seemed to penetrate everyone she looked at like she could see through us. The dress she was wearing was bright blue and rippled like a river.

"Amphitrite," Penny said, disdain in her voice.

"Penelope." The sea goddess responded coldly.

The water seemed to churn more intensely. Whirlpools started forming all around the dining hall. Poseidon snapped his fingers, and the water went back to normal.

"Ladies. Please, let's be civil. We are family after all." He held his hands up in a pleading gesture.

"She tried to kill me." Penny's voice was very quiet but seemed to carry through the room as if she were shouting.

"I understand this. However, my wife would never do that again. Isn't that right Amphitrite?" Poseidon narrowed his eyes at his wife.

"Of course, my lord." Amphitrite bowed then walked to the table, taking a seat next to Rob, keeping an eye on Penny.

Occasionally, she would change her gaze to me. Something about the way she was looking at me made me tense. I couldn't place what the feeling was, but it wasn't right. Poseidon began talking.

"So, as for your transportation, Penny, I have your favorite ship being prepared."

Penny started smiling.

"The Ajax? Really?"

Her father nodded his head.

Penny got up and swam to her father, wrapping him in a hug.

"I thought it was destroyed."

"I found the wreckage and restored it," Poseidon explained, patting his daughter on the back.

"Thank you." She whispered, but I was able to hear it.

While Penny held her father, Amphitrite looked at her, rage in her eyes. I really didn't like how she was looking at Penny. I put my hand under the table and extend my claws, just in case.

Penny let go of her father and swam back to her seat.

"It should be ready soon. I will have more supplies ready for you as well, more arrows for your friend Megan, food, water, and ambrosia."

"Thank you, Lord Poseidon," Blake said, bowing his head.

We finished eating, which was weird with the air bubble around us. It seemed to extend to whatever we were holding.

133

Once our meal was done, Poseidon got up and gestured for us to follow him. We all got up, including Amphitrite, and followed him to the door at the back of the room.

When we went through, we entered another hallway. To our right was another door that seemed to lead to the kitchen. We followed the sea god down the hall, swimming after him. At the end of the hall, there was a huge door that looked like it should be on a shipping dock. Swimming through it, we saw a huge docking area for ships.

There were warships from World War 2, civil warships, pirate ships, and more that I couldn't even recognize. Blake was looking at the warships like he wanted to climb on board and try out all of the weapons. Rachael was checking out the pirate ships like she wanted to know the story behind them.

Poseidon led us down the docks, to the biggest ship of all. It was at least a hundred feet tall, with huge wooden masts. The sails seemed to be made of green silk. Looking at the hull, it was covered with bronze. Portholes covered the side as well. I could see the ends of cannons poking out of the side as well at equal intervals.

We swam to the top of the ship and stepped onto the deck. Mounted on the railings on the side of the ship were huge crossbows like the ones we had at school, at least ten of them. The back end of the ship had what looked like captain's quarters. On top of this area sat the steering wheel. In the middle of the deck was a door, which I assumed led below deck. It was all very impressive.

"Children, may I welcome you aboard the Ajax," Poseidon said.

Penny seemed close to tears. She swam all around, taking in every detail of the ship. She pointed at the sails, and they retracted. The ropes started tying themselves down. Behind us, the captain's quarters door slammed shut.

"Penelope, the Ajax is yours. Your extra supplies are below decks. Good luck, and safe travels." Poseidon said, hugging his daughter one final time.

Penny let go of her father and looked at her stepmother.

"Amphitrite." She said curtly.

"Penelope." The goddess waved her hand and disappeared in a plume of bubbles.

Poseidon raised himself off the deck of the ship. Penny pointed at the rope that was securing the ship to the dock, it untied itself and flew onto the deck. The ship lifted off the ground and shot forward through a set of bay doors.

The ship seemed to be acting as a submarine, possibly due to the power of Poseidon. It cut through the water extremely easily but didn't seem to be taking any damage from being submerged. Penny led the ship straight to the surface. We broke through into the sunlight. It was a little disorienting breathing regular air again, as the magic Poseidon had provided melted away. I noticed a big difference from the magic air Poseidon provided us.

Once we were on the open water Penny released the sails and we coasted on the water at a reasonable pace.

"We're going eighty knots. Roughly 92 miles an hour. The ship is enchanted, so we shouldn't feel the wind." She said, walking up to me.

"How long do you think it will take us to get home?" I asked.

"Maybe a week or so. We have to travel through the Panama Canal. Don't worry." She said, probably because of the look on my face. "We won't have to deal with mortals. My father is simply going to grant us passage there. He's going to open a portal to take us to the other side."

"Sounds good. So, can I ask you something?"

"Of course."

"What's so special about this ship?"

She closed her eyes and took a deep breath.

"There are two answers to that question."

"Okay?"

"First, it's named after my favorite greek hero; Ajax. He fought at the battle of Troy with Achilles. Second, Ajax was my first boyfriend's name."

"The one that was a werewolf?"

She nodded.

"The first time I sailed on this ship was with him." She had a tear in her eyes. "After he went home, I took it out again. I was attacked by a sea serpent. The ship sank. I thought I'd never see it again. That was five years ago, in two thousand eleven."

I stood there thinking for a few moments. Thinking of nothing else to do, I hugged her. A few moments later, she hugged me back. We stood there for a few moments embracing each other until I heard a slight cough from behind me.

Penny and I broke apart and Blake was standing there.

"Penny, we need you."

She nodded and followed Blake to the helm where Megan was waiting for them. Rachael and Rob were standing next to the mast in the middle of the ship. I walked up to them while they were talking. They stopped once Rachael saw me.

"What's up?" I asked.

"Nothing," Rachael answered quickly.

Rob looked at me, his face read: later.

"Okay. Anyway, Penny said it's going to take about a week to get us home." I explained.

"Awesome. A week on a boat. Fun." Rob said sarcastically.

"It's better than walking back." Rachael reasoned.

Rob laughed.

"I'm going to go below deck. Check out the cannons."

Rob walked away, lifted up the door, and descended down the stairs. Rachael looked at me for a few moments.

"So, when we get home, how about we reschedule that date?" She blushed.

"Sure, I don't see a problem with that," I said, honestly.

Maybe that's what I needed to get my mind off of all this godly stuff. Ever since leaving the underworld I kept thinking about my father, and Hades attempt to kill us. Even more so, my mind kept drifting to that force that was trying to lure me into the woods. It gave me a weird chill every time I tried to comprehend it.

A huge smile sprang to Rachael's face after hearing my words. She gave me a quick hug and ran to the helm of the ship where Blake and Megan were standing. Using the winds, I flew up and joined them. Blake was steering the ship while Megan looked over a map.

"Where's Penny?" I asked.

Megan looked up from her map.

"Captain's quarters."

"Right. Is something wrong with the ship?"

"No," Blake answered. "Just wanted an eta and a quick lesson on how to sail this thing."

"Gottcha. I'll be back."

I jumped down to the deck and turned around to the door. Before walking in, I knocked.

"Come in." Said a choked-up voice from inside.

I slowly opened the door. Penny was sitting behind a large wooden desk, her hands wrapped around a small green gem about the size of a quarter.

"You okay?" I asked.

She quickly took a piece of paper off the desk and slid it into a drawer.

"Fine. Just a present from my dad. He left it for me in the desk" Her eyes were bloodshot like she had been crying.

I walked farther into the room and joined her behind the desk, taking in the room. It looked like your typical captain's quarters you would see in a movie. Books lined the walls. Map and globes were scattered on tables. I looked ever Penny's shoulder at the gem.

"What is it?" I asked.

She pushed back softly from the desk and stood. With a look of concentration on her face,

she clutched the gem. As Penny held it, however, it started to glow. A few moments later, in her hand where the gem had been, was now a trident, six feet long. The ends of the weapon were coated with bronze, the shaft was decorated with smaller versions of the original gem.

"Magical trident. Once I start using it more, I should be able to make it change easier."

"That's kind of impractical though, isn't it?" I asked.

"I'm gonna have Rob see what he can do with it."

"Hey, if anyone can make it something better, it's Rob."

Penny laughed and wiped her face with her free hand.

"My dad left a note. It said that the gem, and trident, will also increase my power over water."

"How so?" I sat on the edge of the desk.

"Apparently, instead of just controlling the movements of the water, I can also control the state. So, I can turn it into ice or steam basically."

"That's pretty cool," I admitted.

"Yeah. The other states also gain some godly power too. The waters just water, but the ice is harder than any ice on earth. The steam is hotter than lava. According to my dad."

I looked at her with wide eyes. Penny was already someone I didn't want to mess with. It only took that first sparring session for me to realize that. She normally didn't lose her temper or show her power, but I knew she had endless reserves of it inside her. Add in the ability to trap me in ice I can't break out of, or burn me alive with steam. I didn't want to think about it.

Penny concentrated again and turned her trident back into a gem.

"The crew quarters are below decks. There's definitely more than enough bunks for everyone. You should drop your bag off."

I nodded, taking the hint that she wanted to be alone.

"I'll want you on the first watch with me. If that's okay?" She said as I was walking to the door.

"Sure," I said with a smile.

"Well, good."

I nodded again and walked out on the deck.

When I stepped into the fresh sea air, Rob was just coming up from below deck. I walked by him and descended the steps. Once I was downstairs, I saw a sea of cannons pointing out either side of the ship. Farther down, there was a hallway that seemed to have doors on either side. I walked down the hallway and saw an empty bunk on the right.

It was a simple room, just a bed and a nightstand that held a candle for light. I placed my bag on the bed and sat down.

I wasn't really tired, more just mentally drained. For the first time, everything that had happened began to really sink in. I've met three gods. Two of them were my uncles, the other my aunt. Hades fought me and almost killed me. Poseidon treated me like family, he fed me. Granted, that might be because I'm Penny's friend. Penny and I weren't technically related, and

Poseidon had treated all of my other friends like this. However, the point still stands.

Before I got even more into my thoughts, however, the ship shook. Water splashed up and covered the porthole in my room.

"Jensen!" Megan's voice traveled from upstairs.

I got up and ran for the stairs, taking them two at a time. Throwing open the hatch, I jumped on deck. I spun toward the front of the ship. Penny was standing there, trident in hand, controlling a wave that was smashing into a gigantic sea serpent.

The serpent was like nothing I had ever seen before. Green in color, it loomed at least a hundred feet above the deck. Looking at the monster, I saw its head. Well, heads. Three of them. Each was armed with razor-sharp teeth that looked like they could liquify a dump truck. When it opened its jaws, the creature's mouth looks big enough to swallow an elephant whole.

Megan ran past me and vaulted into the rigging. She climbed until she reached the top of the mast, and notched an arrow. She let it fly and it made contact. However, the arrow simply shattered on the sea serpent scales.

"Jensen! Fry it!" Blake yelled over the crashing of water on the deck.

I pulled my flashlight from my pocket and channeled electricity toward the bulb. Instantly, I held my sword. Running as fast as I could at the monster, I jumped when I reached the bow of the ship. I flew through the air, straight toward the monster's middle head.

Its other heads were ready for me though. The one on the right turned and opened its mouth. Without warning, red-hot fire came billowing from its maw. The left head did the same, but instead of fire, a small blizzard erupted forward.

I used the winds to force myself down, out of the way of the blasts. I flew upwards and stabbed my sword into the middle head's mouth while dodging the heat and cold. The hilt of my sword sank into the roof of the mouth. Quicker than I thought possible, the monster snapped its jaws shut.

I moved my arm out of the way just in time. The middle head opened its mouth again, and I rocketed backward using the wind. My sword was still lodged in the monster's mouth. Fire came soaring out of the right head. I hit the button on my watch and blocked it with my shield.

"Lightning would be good any time!" Rob yelled from the deck, fighting the left head, which was now taking chunks out of the railing.

The sea serpent opened it's middle head again, and I saw the hilt of my sword. Using it as a focal point, I summoned a bolt of lightning from the air. Thunder clapped, and the sea serpent lit up like a Christmas tree. Literally, like a Christmas tree. The beast started glowing red, blue, and green.

A few seconds later, the middle head drooped and slammed backward into the water, waves crashing all around. However, the other two heads were very much active. I looked down and saw my sword floating in the water. Before I could summon it with a wind current, a geyser appeared and lifted it to me.

I looked down at Penny, but her focus was no longer on me. I took the sword from the water and went back to work.

The left head was freezing the cannons on the port side of the ship. On the starboard side, the other head was attempting to set Rob aflame. He was standing there in the blaze without even moving a muscle. As he stood, I saw him look through his pockets. Apparently, he found something that he liked, and took it out, throwing it into the creature's maw.

A few seconds later, I saw a circle appear in the monster's throat. The fire had stopped, and Rob had a smile on his face. He then ran to the port side to fend off the other head.

I was so enthralled with what Rob was doing, I completely forgot about the freezing cannons. The head had now moved on to my friends. I saw it open its mouth, ready to flash freeze them. Using the wind, I hurled myself toward its neck. In one fluid motion, I slammed the edge of my shield as hard as I could.

Sea serpent scales were as hard as diamonds. At least, that's what we learned at school. However, my strike shattered them all, exposing the creature's flesh. My shield, however, did the same and shattered.

"Oh, come on! Now I have to make a new one!" Rob yelled from the deck.

Below me, I heard Penny scream in rage. I looked down and saw her throwing her trident into the sea serpents exposed flesh. The creature hissed in pain. Penny summoned the weapon back to her hand. As the trident exited the serpent's neck, it made a loud squishing sound.

Penny then summoned another geyser of water that hit the monster in it's wound. Before I could even blink, the water circled the serpent's neck and froze. The beast thrashed around, but the ice didn't even crack. Penny threw her trident again, stabbing the monster in its right eye. I flew in with my sword and lopped the serpent's head off, starting at the small amount of exposed flesh. The creature began to dissolve into flame. Penny's trident began to fall to the water, but I dropped down and snatched it out of the air.

"Here you go," I said, landing on the deck and handing it to her.

"Thanks." She responded, changing the weapon back to a gem. "Rob, I think there are some spare wood and bronze below deck. Can you fix the railings?"

"No problem, boss." He ran off down the stairs.

"Rachael, help him if you can. Blake, try to thaw the cannons on the port side."

They both agreed and ran off behind Rob.

"Megan, take the helm. Let me know if we run into any problems."

She nodded, and again, ran to her destination.

Penny and I walked to the captain's quarters. She slid her sword from her belt and placed it on the desk. Walking over to a small alcove on the left side of the room, she sat down on a bed.

"I hate sea serpents." She whispered.

I walked over and sat next to her.

"So do I," I said, lightly bumping into her shoulder.

She smiled but looked exhausted.

"Good moves out there by the way."

I nodded.

"You had some good ones too. You okay?"

She sighed.

"New powers take a little while to get used to. I'll be fine. Just tired."

"Yeah, I know the feeling," I remembered being extremely tired after using my godly powers the first time against the hellhound.

"I'm going to push the ship to its limits. I can keep it together. The less time we're on the sea, the better. I don't want to have to deal with attacks like that too often, but they might be more frequent." Penny said.

"Because of Hades?" I guessed.

"Yeah. I think he can sense us, and I think he's going to send more sea monsters after us. My dad can keep most of them away, but some will slip through."

"Always fun." I laughed.

Penny lay back on her bed.

"I'm going to try to take a nap. Wake me if anything happens?"

"Sure." I got up and walked to the deck, hoping we didn't meet any more sea monsters.

The next stint of the trip was more or less smooth. Penny used her power over water to increase our speed. What would have taken us several days, only took us two. We made it to the Panama Canal in no time. Penny, however, was exhausted from controlling the water for so long.

"The canal is about thirty miles ahead of us. My father said he would open a portal around here." She explained, slowing the ship down to almost a full stop.

"So, what do we look for?" Megan asked.

Penny sat down on the deck, her back against the mast.

"Big green portal. Big enough to sail the ship through."

She took a shell out of her pocket and chucked it over the side of the ship.

"Signal." She said, answering our confused looks.

She closed her eyes and leaned her head back. The rest of us waited for a portal to appear, everyone looking in a different direction.

"There!" Blake yelled after about twenty minutes. He was looking forward, toward the canal.

We all turned. Sure enough, there was a massive green glowing portal in the middle of the water. Penny sighed, and the ship started moving forward again. Using a wind current, I released the sails. The ship moved to the portal, and a few moments later, we were on the other side.

The water was the same color, but Penny got up, looking a little refreshed.

"The waters a little cleaner here. I'm going for a dip. Jensen, keep a gust of wind on the sails. I'll catch up."

Without another word, she ran to the port side of the ship and jumped over. I heard a distinct splash. The rest of us walked around the ship. Rob brought up some food from the galley. He, Rachael and I sat on the deck around the mast, waiting for Penny to resurface. As we did so, I summoned a consistent wind current pressed against the sails, and we picked up the pace.

"So, Jensen. We've been friends and have known each other for over a month now." Rob said.

"Yeah?"

"I want more werewolf info, man!"

"Like what?" I asked, confused.

"Like, backstory. Are there different types of you?"

"Well, you know the general backstory about Lycaon and Zeus and stuff."

"Naturally," Rachael added.

I took a bite of a ham sandwich.

"As far as types go, yeah, there's a few."

Rob made a waving motion like: go on.

"There are alphas, which are the leaders of the pack," I explained. "Then there's deltas.

They're sort of like the second in charge in case the alpha dies."

"Like your Uncle Jack?" Rachael asked.

I nodded, trying not to feel jealous.

"Then there are betas. That's me. Just a member of the pack. After them, there are omegas. Lone wolves. They have no pack. They're super weak, compared to betas."

"Why's that?" Rachael questioned.

"Generally, werewolves are stronger together." I took a sip of soda. "Not just the numbers factor. We literally get stronger if there's more of us around. Right now, my max I can lift is around thirty tons when I'm fully shifted. When I'm with my pack, that's almost tripled."

"So, omegas are weaker because they're on their own?" Rob asked.

"Correct, my friend. Omegas can gather together, and they get strength from that, but they aren't actually a pack, so it's not as good. Only an alpha can bring an omega into a pack."

Rachael nodded.

"What about the originals? Are they still around?" Rob leaned forward a little.

"Yeah. The Immortals. They're the last type. They're the ones that turn into giant wolves. As far as I know, they're the most powerful, and they're still around. No one knows where though."

"I heard a story, a long time ago, that there were werewolf sightings in New York." Rachael offered.

"Could have been my pack or a rival pack. Could have been the Immortals. No idea."

Before we could continue our conversation, a column of water erupted on the starboard side. Penny walked out onto the deck, completely dry. She did not look happy.

"Feel better?" Rob asked.

"Physically, yes. Mentally, no. There's an army of sea monsters five miles up."

She pointed at the sails and the wheel, turning both of them. The ship began to turn, and we picked up even more speed. As we sailed, Penny began to look more relaxed.

After about three hours of sailing at top speed, Penny looked over the side of the ship. She heaved a sigh of relief.

"We're in the clear. Two more days at this speed, and we should be home."

Penny was right. She did her best to avoid sea monsters. Every now and then we were attacked by a small sea serpent or giant crab, but for the most part, we sailed safely. Penny steered us through the Gulf of Saint Lawrence in Canada and followed the river down into Lake Erie.

We sailed for the rest of the day, letting Penny and I rest from keeping the ship going at full speed for two whole days with no sleep. Once we cleared the lake, Blake steered the ship into the harbor. According to Penny and Rachael, the school had a dock here, though it was normally empty.

Once the ship had docked and was secured, we walked out on to land for the first time in days. It felt good. Penny, however, seemed extremely reluctant to get off the ship.

"Penny, you coming?" I yelled up to her from the dock.

"Yeah." She yelled back, and finally climbed down the rope ladder.

"You okay?" I asked when she caught up to me.

"Just going to miss it. The ship I mean."

I furrowed my eyebrows.

"It's still going to be there, isn't it? So you can see it at any time?"

Penny shook her head, stopped, and pointed behind us. Right before my eyes, the ship was already starting to dissolve into a white mist, returning to the sea.

"Dad keeps his ships at home. That way, nothing happens to them."

"Where exactly is his palace?" I asked as we started walking again.

It was unclear. I know we emerged from the Pacific Ocean, but where Poseidon's kingdom was, I had no idea.

"It's physical location is in the Atlantic. Close to Mount Olympus. However, he can make it appear in any ocean. Hence why it was in the Pacific." She explained.

I nodded. We had now caught up with our friends. Sadly, we still had a short walk ahead of us, but compared to everything else we had been through, that seemed easy.

Finally, about an hour later, we were home.

14

Chapter Fourteen: Peace, for now

As we walked out of the forest and through the main gates of the school, several students ran to greet us. I recognized Andrew, the head of Hermes dorm. He made straight for Rachael, taking her bag and started talking her ear off.

"What's that about?" I whispered to Penny.

"They're pretty good friends. He knows that her cousin is one of his brothers. Always asks if she saw him while she was on a quest." She answered.

We walked farther on the grounds. A few of Penny's siblings came to greet her. Rob took off to the forges, Blake to the armory. Megan ran off to join her siblings on the archery range behind the school. I stood there, alone. Before I could make up my mind on what I wanted to do, Leonardo came walking out of the front doors of the school.

"Jensen!" He had his arms open in greeting.

"Hi, Leo." I walked up to him.

"Penny's father sent word that you would be returning. I take it everything went well?" He had a huge smile on his face, and I really didn't want to see it go away.

"We should probably go to your office."

I whistled to Rachael, who was standing next to the east wall, talking to a few of her sisters. She motioned to them that she would be back and ran to join Leo and I. As we walked, no one talked. Rachael looked over her shoulder as we crossed the threshold of the school. I followed her gaze to Penny, who was watching us intensely. Once she saw that I was looking, she looked away and began talking to one of her brothers.

Leo led Rachael and me into his office. We took our places in the chairs in front of his desk. I looked around at the office, the same library of books sat on the shelves. On the desk, however, was a new addition.

Leo had a map of the school laid out on his desk, differently colored miniature statues littered the school grounds. There was a color for each one of the dorms. I noticed one sky blue figure at the back of the map. I looked at Leo quizzically.

"I was planning for the battle. Keeping you at the back, as you can see, for support."

"Well, chances are you won't need that plan, Leonardo," Rachael said.

Rachael and I took turns explaining our quest. She filled in the parts I wasn't around for, mainly because I was either unconscious, or blown out of a volcano. I filled in for her, like with my fight with Hades. By the end of our tale, about an hour later, Leo was just looking at us, a proud look on his face.

"Well, from the sounds of it, we shouldn't be attacked by Hades any time soon."

"That's what I thought," Rachael said. "However, some of the dragons survived. Plus, Hades now has it out for Jensen even more. He might work to make his monsters rise faster, or worse."

Leo nodded.

"I have the same thought. Hades realm is directly above Tartarus. He does have some sway in the way monsters reform. However, since Tartarus himself hates the gods, it is unlikely he will assist in reforming more powerful beings."

"Wait, Tartarus is alive?" I asked, confused.

"Correct." Leo nodded. "His body is the pit where all monsters go to reform."

"The Titans and most of the giants are held prisoner there," Rachael added.

"Speaking of giants," Leo said. "You mentioned you faced the giant Damysus?"

Rachael and I nodded.

"That may pose a long-term problem."

"What do you mean?" I questioned.

"It sounds like the sons of Gaea are rising. Which is good for no one. In all honesty, I'm very surprised you were able to kill him. In ancient times, it took the power of Chiron the centaur and Apollo to kill him."

"Chiron, the guy who trained Achilles?" I asked.

Leo nodded.

"He stops by every now and then for some hardcore training. He's actually a really nice guy." Rachael said.

"Noted." That list in my head just kept getting longer, even though I hadn't added to it in days.

"However, the immediate threat would still be Hades," Leo said, bringing us back on track. "The meeting of the gods is taking place tomorrow. Zeus and Poseidon are obviously not happy with their brother. The other gods, however, are yet to be determined."

"So, what you're telling me is that we can still be attacked?" I pondered.

"Correct, Jensen, but I have a plan."

Rachael and I sat still, ready to listen.

"I'm going to send your party to Olympus to provide details and plead for assistance. Hades cannot set his plan into motion."

"How are we going to get there?" This time it was Rachael asking the question. "Olympus is closed during a council."

"The main entrance in D.C. is, correct. However, I'm going to send you through the gate."

No one said anything for a few moments.

"Not the gate. Anyway but the gate." Rachael whispered, her head down and her eyes closed.

"What's the gate?" I asked, thoroughly out of my depth.

"The gate, Jensen, is the only other way into Olympus for mortals. It is protected by Heracles. You may know him by his Roman name; Hercules. However, some don't make it back." Leo's eyes gravitated to Rachael, who was silently crying now. "Rachael's other cousin attempted to enter Olympus this way. He, sadly, didn't make it back."

"What does Heracles do? Why is it so dangerous?"

"Heracles will challenge you. Not only is he the gatekeeper of Olympus, but he is also the god of strength and of sports, he could challenge you to a contest of either, or sometimes both."

"I think I can handle the strength part, Leo." I joked.

"I'm not sure about that Jensen. Heracles is the strongest god when it comes to weight. I'm not sure even your considerable strength can match him."

"I'm going to find out." I was sure of that. "When do we leave?"

"Tomorrow morning. The council will be held at noon. You'll be leaving at five in the morning. I was able to procure you a car from town. I will be driving you, however, I cannot join you. I'll simply be dropping you off on the outskirts of D.C. where the gates are located."

"Awesome," I said. I wasn't looking forward to relaxing or anything. I thought.

Rachael and I got up.

"We'll let everyone else know," Rachael said, choking back her words, tears still in her eyes.

As we walked out, I put my arm around her shoulders. Once we were in the entrance hall, the front doors opened. Penny and Rob were walking in. I quickly took my arm off of Rachael's shoulders.

"What's up?" Penny asked.

I explained to her and Rob everything Leo said and what we had to do. Rachael stood next to me, gaining her composer. When I was done, Penny just nodded.

"Well, it sounds like you're going to have your work cut out for you, buddy," Rob said, patting me on the back.

"Yeah. So, I'm thinking we should all take the rest of the day, sleep, recuperate, and get ready. I don't know what Heracles is going to have us do."

"I agree." Penny offered. "I'll inform Blake and Megan."

I nodded and Penny ran off outside. Rob followed, heading to the forges. Rachael and I stood alone again.

"You okay?" I asked after a few moments of silence.

"Fine." She said, straightening up, her eyes still red.

"Are you going to be able to handle this tomorrow?"

"I don't have a choice." She sighed. "Right now, I just want to sleep."

"I'll fly you upstairs."

Rachael and I walked to the base of the stairs and using the winds, I flew us to her floor. When we landed, she said goodbye and gave me a hug.

"See you in the morning." She said and walked into her dorm.

I flew to my own floor and walked into my dorm. Throwing my bag on the couch, I walked up the stairs into my room and flopped down on my bed. I hadn't realized how tired I was. Instantly, I fell asleep.

I don't really remember what my dream was. Something about giant marble columns and a flying eagle.

However, I was awoken to a banging on my dormitory door. I heard Penny yelling.

"Jensen! It's four in the morning, time to get ready!"

I rolled out of bed and rubbed my eyes. The sun wasn't even close to being up yet. I quickly walked to the bathroom and took a shower. Once I was dressed, I took the dirty clothes, and the money I had left, out of my bag and pocketed the cash.

Sliding my flashlight back into my pocket, I walked out of my dorm and jumped over the banister. When I hit the ground, on top of a cushion of air, all of my friends along with Leo were standing there.

"About time." Rob joked. "Penny, I was able to do what you wanted."

Out of his pocket, he pulled a ring with a small green gem encased by a thin layer of bronze. I recognized that it was the same gem Penny had on the Ajax.

"You did it that quick?" She asked, taking the ring and sliding it onto her right hand.

"I work magic, my friend." Rob smiled, clearly proud of himself. "Should work and look the same way it used to. Encased in a little godly bronze I had leftover from a birthday present from dad." He explained.

"Thank you, so much." Penny walked up and hugged him.

"No problem," Rob said, patting her back.

Leo cleared his throat.

"We must be going." He said, jingling his car keys. "If you don't mind."

We followed Leo out of the front doors. Right outside of the gates was a black SUV. I noticed a bronze motorcycle was connected to the back on top of a trailer.

"Bringing it along just in case. It's finally done." Rob said, answering my confused look.

Once that was explained, we all piled into the SUV.

The car was actually pretty roomy. I had enough room to extend and relax even with Penny and Rob on either side of me in the farthest back row of seats.

Once Leo drove out through a small path in the woods and onto the highway, Rob passed out and started snoring.

I looked over at Penny and she was looking at the ring on her finger.

"Everything okay?" I asked.

"Just marveling at the work Rob did."

"It is really pretty. Matches your eyes." I commented.

Penny turned and looked at me.

"Shut up, flyboy." She joked, lightly pumping me with her shoulder.

Everyone chatted while we drove, except Rob, who slept the entire time. Rachael pointed out landmarks as we went and gave us a brief description of their history. Blake chimed in every now and then with a random remark on a battle that happened during the revolutionary war. Apparently, demigods fought on both sides. George Washington was a son of Poseidon according to Blake. I guess that's why it was so easy for him to cross the Delaware River in the middle of winter.

In what seemed like no time at all, Leo was slowing the car down. He took a turn down a dusty road, roughly thirty miles outside of D.C. He drove for a few minutes, then pulled the car over. There were a good two miles of fields on either side of us.

Leo took a deep breath.

"Walk about a mile into the field on our right. From there, you'll see two giant marble pillars. After that, it's up to Heracles."

We all nodded, suddenly serious.

As everyone got out of the car, I shook Rob until he woke up.

"What?" He asked, obviously agitated.

"We're here. You've been asleep for six hours." Penny informed him.

"Sorry," Rob said, getting out of the car and stretching.

Once Penny and I had gotten out, Leonardo rolled down the window.

"Be safe. I imagine that you'll receive transport home when all is said and done." He told us.

"If we survive," Rachael whispered. No one seemed to hear her but me. When she caught my eye, she blushed and looked scared.

Rob detached his bike from the back of the SUV and walked it into the field where it was covered with wheat. With that Leo pulled the car around and drove off, dust billowing in his wake.

"Well, let's get going," Penny ordered.

No one said anything for a while as we walked. We were on too high of an alert. The sun was just about to be overhead. According to my watch, it was just after eleven. Apparently, Leo drove extremely fast. How he was able to not get pulled over, I have no idea.

After about ten minutes of silence, Rob finally spoke up.

"So, Jensen, you know we're about to meet your brother right?" He said, his hands casually entwined behind his head.

To be honest, the thought didn't occur to me. Heracles was a god, but he did use to be a demigod. A son of Zeus.

"Never even thought about that."

"I've heard he can lift mountains," Blake said. "He's never been bested in a show of strength by a mortal."

"Good to know," I mumbled, my spirits lowering.

How was I going to beat him in a strength contest if he was that strong? I shook my head to clear out the thoughts. If I was going to think like that, I might as well just run home now.

Before anyone else could say anything else about Heracles, however, Rachael stopped us, pointing ahead.

"There." She said softly.

Sure enough, roughly three hundred yards ahead of us were two, thirty feet high marble pillars. In between, stood a man. From this distance, I could tell he was wearing a normal white Greek tunic. Over his shoulder lay an orange fur. His eyes were the same color as mine; sky blue. He looked as if he could crush rocks in his hands, which he probably could. The guy was seriously ripped. A slight breeze blew, and his black hair flew around his face.

"What's that over his shoulder?" Megan asked.

"Probably the Nemean Lion's fur. His spoil of war from when he killed the monster." Rachael said.

I remembered the story. Heracles was set to complete twelve labors after being sent crazy by Hera, who was tormenting him. His first task was to kill the Nemean Lion; a giant lion with unbreakable fur. Heracles only managed to kill it by trapping it and strangling it. Impressive.

I noticed that we had been standing there for quite a while. Heracles hadn't moved.

"Let's go." I said and started walking toward my godly brother.

"Stop!" A deep voice echoed when we were twenty feet away.

I stopped dead in my tracks. The voice definitely came from Heracles. He stood there and a smile crept across his face.

"Demigods!" He said happily, his voice was much quieter now. "I take it you are here for entrance to Olympus?"

Penny looked like she was about to speak, but I stopped her.

"Yes," I said. "We must meet with the Olympians during the council."

"Oh yes, my father said that some demigods would be stopping by. Leonardo sent him a message last night." Heracles explained.

"That's good. So, how do we gain entrance?"

Heracles reached down and picked a massive club from the ground. I really didn't want to see him use it. If even half of his stories were true, this was one dangerous guy.

He walked toward us, still smiling. As he got closer, I could feel his power radiating over me. It wasn't as strong as Hades' but I had the feeling that he could kill us any time he wanted.

Once Heracles was two feet from me, he took a very deep breath through his nose.

"Well now, that's a change of pace. Another son of Zeus! Brother!" He

153

wrapped his arms around me, but I didn't return the favor.

Locked in this awkward hug, I could feel Heracles' strength. Even when he wasn't trying to, he almost cracked my ribs. When he let me go, I resisted the urge to rub my side.

As he looked over me, Heracles took another sniff of air.

"Is that, what is it? Dog?" He questioned.

"Werewolf, actually," Penny said protectively.

"Oh." Heracles sounded kind of disappointed. "That's right. You're dads little, let's say, misfortune. You're causing him a lot of problems, brother."

"I wouldn't know. He doesn't talk to me." I said with a slight hint of anger.

"To be fair, Zeus has never been a great dad. Always distant. He didn't talk to me until I died." Heracles said, changing his grip on his club.

"Good to know," I whispered.

"Now, as far as going to Olympus is concerned. If it were up to me, because you're family, I'd let you through no problem."

"Awesome!" Rob said. "So, you just wave your hand and we go through some pearly gates?"

Heracles cleared his throat.

"I said, son of Hephaestus if it were up to me. Sadly, it's not. Sometimes I can pull strings, but, because it's you, brother, I can't. Plus, I don't very much like your friend here." He pointed his club at Penny.

"The feelings mutual." She said. I got what she meant, he seemed like your typical frat boy. I hate frat boys.

"Children of Zeus and Poseidon generally don't get along. If I were you, Jensen, I would find some better company."

"My company is just fine," I told him. Who was he to talk about Penny like that?

"If you say so. Now, what kind of contest should I offer you?"

Heracles slowly paced around, scratching his head and muttering to himself. I couldn't make out any words, but I don't even think he was saying real words.

After about five minutes of pacing, Heracles stopped in his tracks and snapped his fingers.

"I got it! I've never been in a lifting contest with a werewolf. So, that's what we'll do! If you beat me, you and your friends go through my gates." He snapped his fingers again.

In between the marble columns, two huge bronze gates formed and glittered in the sun.

"How does that sound?" My godly brother asked.

This is the last thing I wish he would have challenged me too, but did I have a choice?

"One condition," I said, my brain working quickly. I really didn't trust this guy. "You swear on the River Styx that you will let us through if I win. No detours, no tricks."

Heracles rolled his eyes.

"I swear on the River Styx." He said, annoyance in his voice. Thunder boomed from above. "So, we have a deal?"

"Deal."

Once the words left my mouth, Heracles waved his hand. Next to us, two sets of weights and a barbell appeared.

"The weights are enchanted by me. We'll lift increasingly large amounts. After each lift, I'll change the weight. Deadlifts only." He smiled, obviously, he was excited about this.

Heracles walked over to the weights on the right. Before I took my spot on the left, Penny grabbed my hand.

"Be careful. I don't trust him." She whispered in my ear.

I nodded and took my spot behind my barbell.

"Let's start it off light, shall we?" Heracles said, snapping his fingers.

I looked down at my weights. The numbers on the side changed. At first, they just had a double zero. Now, however, they showed one ton.

Heracles bent down and gripped his barbell with one hand. In one fluid motion, he lifted the weight above his head and held it there for five seconds.

"Your turn." He said as he dropped the weight to the ground.

"Easy," I said, and picked the barbell up and held it the same way the god did.

When I let the weight drop, Heracles just looked at me.

"Let's take it up a notch." He snapped his fingers again, and the weights changed to five tons.

Again, my divine brother picked up the weight one-handed and held it for a five-count. I copied him. When I dropped the weight this time, Heracles' mouth was hanging open.

"No one can lift that much but me." He was shocked.

"Well, I guess you were wrong." I boasted.

Heracles looked angry now. When he snapped his fingers again, the weights increased to ten tons.

That's my limit while I'm human. I thought. I really didn't want to shift.

Despite my reservations about shifting, I lifted the weight with both hands and held it above my head for a five-count. That was apparently the wrong move. When the barbell hit the ground, Heracles did not look happy. He snapped his fingers and now in front of me lay a twenty-ton weight.

"Let's see you lift this."

The god bent over and gripped the barbell with both hands. He seemed to struggle a little but was able to get it up.

Without even thinking I went into a full shift. Heracles said nothing, but stood there and watched. I used two hands as well and lifted the barbell above my head with ease. The next time Heracles snapped his fingers, the numbers on the weights shot directly to fifty tons. I couldn't help but let my worry show in my face.

"Too much for you, brother?"

I heard the god's weight hit the ground. When I looked up, Heracles actually had sweat on his face. Could gods sweat?

Looking over at my friends, I made eye contact with Penny.

"You can do this." She whispered so quietly only I could hear her.

I bent over and grabbed the barbell. Putting everything I had into it, I managed to get it off the ground.

"No!" Heracles yelled.

There was a clap of thunder, but I kept my grip, raising the weight higher and higher. Right around my waist, I felt my strength give out. I couldn't lift it any higher. Sweat began pouring down my face and back. Soaking through my shirt. However, my brother had made up his mind.

In his rage, Heracles had lifted his club and threw it towards my friends. In a blink of an eye, several things happened.

First, I heard Penny yell in pain. Second, I felt pure rage and lifted the weight above my head. Finally, Heracles was knocked backward by my barbell.

He picked it up and threw it aside with a great deal of effort.

"You werewolves! I knew there was a reason we all hated you! Thinking you're stronger than a god!" He bellowed.

I looked over and saw Penny bleeding from the head, laying on the ground. Megan was kneeling next to her, her medical bag opened on the ground.

"I out lifted you, Heracles. You hurt my friend. That was a bad idea. First, you're going to open the gates. Second, you better pray to dad that she's okay, or you are not going to have a good time." I told my brother.

I ran over to Penny and grabbed her hand. I could feel my blood pumping through my veins. My heart was racing. Rage was filling my head.

"Is she going to be okay?" I asked Megan.

"I don't know. It's a pretty bad crack in the skull."

I heard the gates behind me open. When I looked around at my friends, they all had their weapons out.

"Stand down. I've got this." I ordered.

I stood up and spun to face Heracles.

"The gates will be open for five minutes. You can use that time to fight me, or take your friend inside to receive help." Heracles said.

"Get her inside," I told my friends.

I didn't bother to wait for an answer. I was so angry that I just acted.

Heracles summoned his club back to his hand. I yelled and the winds spun around me like a cyclone. Lightning hit the ground all around me. When I ran, I knew Heracles didn't stand a chance.

He swung his club around. It made contact a few times, but I paid it no attention, even as my bones broke. My claws moved like the wind, my fangs sank into each inch of the god they could reach as my rage and werewolf instincts took control. The smell of ozone filled the air as lightning continued to hit the ground and my enemy.

A few moments later, all was calm. I looked down and saw the god of strength lying on the ground, silver ichor pooling around his body. He lifted his head.

"Not bad for a half breed. You better hope father doesn't react to this."

Before I could respond Heracles body dissolved into white dust and was carried away on the wind. The only thing left of him was his orange lion's skin. I picked it up. It felt like normal fur, but I could tell it was strong. It had no marks on it, even after my attack on its original owner. Without a thought, I threw the lions pelt into the wind. It was carried off into the distance by the wind.

I turned toward the bronze gates, which were now slowly closing. I ran to meet my friends.

15

Chapter Fifteen: Oh, hi dad

When I stepped through the gate I was immediately met by a blinding white light. I felt as if I was walking through a field of clouds. A light breeze was brushing my skin. However, after a few steps, the sensation was gone. My vision cleared.

In front of me was a glowing city. When I looked around, I saw gardens that held minor gods who were sitting and talking. Houses stood magnificently all around. The light glow that was emanating from everything cut the need for lights. Saytrs ran around carrying trays of ambrosia. Fountains were scattered around the gardens. The sky was black, constellations faintly glowing in the distance. A road stretched out in front of me. I absorbed all of this in a few seconds before I snapped back to reality.

When I looked down, Penny's head was being clutched in the lap of Rachael. Megan was looking through her bag with haste. Blood was still pouring from the wound on Penny's head. Blake and Rob were looking around. Rob was trying to get the attention of the minor gods in the garden, but he was being ignored.

Megan stopped looking through her bag.

"I don't have anything. The bleeding won't stop. She won't eat ambrosia because she's knocked out." She looked at me, pleading for an idea. "Can you change her? You would heal from this no problem."

I shook my head sadly.

"No, only alpha or delta werewolves can change a human. I'm only a beta." I felt useless to her.

I knelt next to Penny and took her hand. She was cold from blood loss. I focused my hearing to catch her heartbeat. It was slowing down. Every beat, Penny was closer to death. My eyes started to sting. When I looked at Rachael, she was fully breaking down.

"I have no ideas. After all of my studying and all of my wisdom, I can't save my best friend." she croaked.

Next, I looked at Megan. Then it clicked.

I shot to my feet and gathered as much air into my lungs as possible.

"APOLLO!"

My shout echoed across Olympus. Windows on the houses nearest us shook.

There were a few moments of silence, which was only broken by Rachael's sobs. Then, there was another blinding light, as if the sun was racing towards me.

"You called?" Apollo asked.

"Father!" Megan squeaked.

Apollo, the god of music, archery, and a whole lot of other things. However, the only thing I cared about was the fact he was the god of medicine. Apollo himself was just a few inches taller than me, maybe six-five at most. His eyes glowed the same color as the sun. He was a good-looking guy, like someone you would see at a coffee shop about to read some slam poetry. Surprisingly, he had on normal clothes; a simple yellow tee-shirt with jeans and sneakers.

"Apollo," I said, wasting no time. "My lord, you are the god of medicine. Please, heal our friend."

Apollo looked down at Penny, who was growing increasingly pale with every passing minute.

"I am the god of many things, Jensen Smith. Prophecies, archery, poetry, art. Perhaps you would like for me to paint you a masterpiece?" Apollo snapped his fingers, and a paintbrush appeared.

The guy was seriously ADD.

"Father. Please, heal my friend." Megan begged.

160

Considering Megan's considerable abilities, I was very surprised that she wasn't able to help Penny herself.

"My precious daughter," Apollo said, his voice ringing slightly. "I tell that you forgot shaved unicorn horn. Which, of course, would heal your friend's wounds. Easy mistake, and I do not fault you for it. Very rare that you require such medicine. Takes up too much space."

"Father!" Megan pleaded. "Please!"

"Oh, I'm very sorry." Apollo smiled, and his teeth were blindingly white. Like looking into the headlights of a car. "As you know, my dear, I do get distracted easily."

No kidding. I thought.

Apollo knelt next to Penny.

"Please, if you don't mind, child." He said to Rachael, gently taking Penny's head from her arms.

Rachael let go and stood up, moving next to me. She locked my arm in a vice grip

"Very easy for me to heal," Apollo whispered.

He waved his hand over Penny's head. Instantly, the wound on her head closed. Color rushed to her face. A few seconds later, Penny took a deep breath and her eyes snapped open.

She looked around and her eyes landed on Apollo.

"How do you feel?" The sun god asked her.

"F-fine, my lord." She made to stand up. Apollo placed a hand on her shoulder.

"Rest for a few moments, child. There is no rush. The council will not take place unless I am present." He stood and turned to look at me. "Our father won't be happy, but I feel sure he will understand my lateness. Considering that I was helping my favorite brother." He smiled again.

Favorite brother? I've never even met him before. How could I be his favorite? Also, it was weird that I was his brother, to begin with. Again, the godly family tree is complicated.

"I love anything that causes father a headache, hence why I like Athena so much. Well, most of the time." He smiled at Rachael.

I looked at Penny. She seemed to be a lot better. Her head was completely healed and all of her colors returned. Slowly, she got to her feet. I walked over to her and gave her some support.

"You okay?" I asked, grabbing her hand and elbow.

"Fine. Just a little groggy." She tried to gently pull away and stumbled.

"I've got you. Don't worry." I said, catching her.

"We need to get to the council," Blake said.

"Of course!" Apollo agreed. "Follow me!"

Megan's dad took off at a brisk jog. However, for a god, that was a full sprint for anyone but me. I picked Penny up and gave her a piggyback ride. Apollo led us down the road that went straight through Olympus. The road was just paved stone blocks like you might see in an ancient city. We passed more houses and gardens. As we passed, minor gods would stare, but avoid us.

Apollo stopped right in front of a set of giant oak doors at the end of the road. My friends and I skidded to a halt behind him. Penny slid off my back.

"Young demigods, I'm pleased to present, the throne room of the gods." Apollo pushed the doors open.

Inside, there was a magnificent throne room. Can you call it a room when it's the size of three basketball courts?

All around the room were thrones at least twenty feet tall. Each one was decorated differently. One was red and embedded with dragons and swords. Another was blue with owls and shields. My eyes settled on the throne that was pure white and engraved with lightning bolts. In the thrones, sat the gods.

The throne I was looking at held a man, thirty feet tall, with salt and pepper hair down to his shoulders. He had a beard that was the same color as his hair. His eyes were a deep blue. I felt his power the entire way across the room. Electricity crackled around him.

"Come in," Apollo whispered, and walked over to his throne, which was yellow and engraved with bows, arrows, harps, and a bunch of other stuff. Megan's dad enlarged and sat down.

My friends and I walked in. Penny was still holding my hand for support.

Apparently, she was still a little light-headed.

We walked into the middle of the throne room. The floor echoed deeply with each step. None of the gods reacted to us. Well, none except Aphrodite.

The goddess had to be one of the most beautiful women I have ever seen. Weirdly, she seemed to look a little like Penny. I pushed that thought aside. Aphrodite was looking directly at Penny and me with a huge smile on her face. Her eyes darted between us and Rachael.

When we reached the middle of the room, all of us knelt in front of Zeus, our heads bowed. I helped Penny down.

"Lord Zeus," Rachael said. "We are here to request assistance against Hades." She sounded a little scared but made eye contact with the king of the gods.

"I know why you are here Rachael Sage." My father's voice boomed through the throne room. The floor shook as the words washed over us.

There was silence in the room for a few moments before Zeus continued.

"Athena. What is your guidance on this matter?" He said, addressing the woman sitting in the owl throne.

Athena had the same long black hair has Rachael. Her eyes were cold and calculating. They glowed with a dim deep blue. Her face was beautiful but seemed to contain a constant scowl.

"Father, I believe we should assist our children, as I have shared with you before. Failure to do so would result in great casualties and could possibly lead to Hades attempting an attack on Olympus." Athena said, her voice was extremely calm and convincing.

Someone cleared his throat on the opposite side of the throne room.

"Ares?" Zeus said.

A god that had a military-style haircut, sunglasses, and scars across his face, sat a little straighter in his throne. When I looked at him, I suddenly got angry, close to violence.

"We all know I hate to agree with Athena," Ares said, a growl in his voice. "However, she is right. Strategically, if Hades were to launch an attack on our children at the Ithaca school, and succeed, he could then attack us. If he does so, he could potentially receive help from more power and ancient beings, such as the Titans."

At the word Titans, the room seemed to grow colder. It was like a shared, unpleasant memory lingered in the air.

"Also, I would hate to see my children dead." A familiar voice said.

Poseidon was sitting on Zeus' right. His sea-green eyes were scanning Penny and I. He sat in a throne the same color as his eyes. It was engraved with tridents and different types of fish. He was dressed the same way I had seen him a few days ago.

Zeus cleared his throat.

"Yes, brother, I see your point." He sounded like he had a note of hatred in his voice. I made a mental note to ask Penny about that later.

The other gods whispered amongst each other.

"Silence," Zeus ordered. The talking stopped instantly. "Jensen Smith. My son. What say you?"

I looked at Penny, who nodded her head, encouraging me to stand. When I stood, I could feel the eyes of everyone in the room. I thought the power washing over me would be enough to make me explode.

"Father, I have seen Hades army myself. I have fought the lord of the Underworld myself. He very much wants to kill me."

I then explained to the gods of our journey in the Underworld and our trip there. I explained my fight with Hades, our battle with Damysus. When explaining the griffin attack, Zeus looked a little disgruntled. I left out the part of sensing werewolves and the force that called me to the forest. Talking in front of all of the gods was nerve-rattling. Finally, my story was done.

"That settles it." Said a new voice. I looked around and saw a man with a winged helmet, short blonde hair and light grey eyes talking. "If we kill this werewolf, then Hades will not attack Ithaca"

"That's not true Hermes," Apollo said. "I have seen a version of the future. Even if young Jensen is killed now, Hades would still want revenge against the others for destroying his palace." Apollo smiled at me.

"My twin is correct." Said the woman sitting directly next to Apollo. Her throne was silver and covered with crescent moons and more bows. "While hunting the Manticore, I felt more dangerous monsters rising." Her gaze turned to me for a few moments. "Hades is preparing more forces, even now, while healing from his battle with our brother."

It was seriously weird being related to all of these powerful gods and goddesses. It made my head hurt.

"Thank you, Artemis," Apollo said graciously.

"Hera, my wife, what is your opinion?" Zeus asked the goddess next to him.

This woman was possibly the most beautiful of them all, aside from Aphrodite. Her flowing brown hair draped her face perfectly. Her purple eyes seemed like they were piercing my soul.

"Well, my love, although I would enjoy seeing the demigod dead, I have to agree with the others. Saving the school is the best course of action. Even though I have no demigod children myself, I cannot allow our family to be picked apart."

"Finally, Demeter, Hephaestus, Dionysus, Aphrodite?" Zeus said.

A bearded man with a rough-looking face and grease-stained hands spoke next. His throne was fire red and engraved with anvils and gears.

"I would hate to see all of my son's creations dismantled." His voice was raspy but kind.

"As would I, hate to see so many plants and crops burned." Said a goddess with wheat-colored hair and eyes. She sat upon a throne engraved with hay and barrels of wheat.

"I'm indifferent." A chubby man with short blonde hair said, spilling wine out of his goblet. "Oops. My apologies father." He snapped his hands and the wine flew from the floor back into his cup. Gross.

"I'd hate to see young love die," Aphrodite said, looking directly at me again and smiling.

Zeus took a deep breath and knit his fingers below his chin. He looked at me up and down, then looked at my friends. When he scanned the room, the other gods avoided his gaze.

I tried to listen for a heartbeat, but I couldn't catch anything. Did gods even have hearts? Another question for later.

My friends were still kneeling and I suddenly felt very aware that I was the only person in the room standing.

Two full minutes had passed, and Zeus still hadn't said anything. Finally, he cleared his throat. Thunder boomed in the distance.

"We will disrupt Hades' army." He said, and a huge weight I hadn't noticed I was carrying fell from my shoulders.

"Thank you, father," I said, kneeling again.

The other gods didn't say anything. They simply sat there, waiting.

"The council is dismissed. Thank you all for your time." Thunder boomed again in the distance.

All around the room, there were pops like sets of firecrackers going off. Different colored lights flashed. Soon, the only remaining gods in the room were our parents; Poseidon, Ares, Athena, Apollo, Hephaestus, and finally, Zeus.

The gods had shrunk back down to human size. They all stood a little taller than me. They walked up to us, mostly smiling.

Athena walked directly to Rachael and wrapped her in a hug. Apollo was going through Megan's medical bag and adding random supplies, talking to her in hushed tones. Hephaestus was marveling at Rob's watch and talking to him about his motorcycle. Ares was patting Blake on the back while Blake was pantomiming a sword slash. Poseidon was fussing over Penny, pouring what smelled like saltwater over her head.

Zeus however, stood next to me awkwardly. It was a full minute until he spoke.

"Follow me, Jensen."

My father led me fifty feet away from the others. I leaned against the nearest throne, which happened to be Apollo's.

"Jensen, I know that I have not been there for you, or your mother." He said suddenly. "And I am very sorry for that. I was extremely fond of your mother."

I just stared at him. How could he be saying this?

"You're the king of the gods. You can do whatever you want." I said coldly.

Zeus sighed.

"Alas, I wish that were true. As it stands, I am on the verge of losing my throne."

"Because of me." I guessed.

166

Zeus hesitantly put his hand on my shoulder.

"No, Jensen. It is my doing. I broke my own oath. My own law."

I furrowed my brow. He was really starting to make me angry.

"I do not regret my actions," Zeus said, reading the look on my face. "You are, by far, the greatest thing I have created in recent memory." Zeus actually smiled.

This time, I'm the one who sighed.

"I do have a few questions."

Zeus seemed to cheer up a little.

"Ask away, my son."

"How did you meet my mom? Why did you break the oath?"

My father looked over my head. He seemed to be staring into the past itself.

"Your mother was out hunting one night. I was on a stroll around a forest in Pennsylvania. Your mother attempted to attack me, thinking I was an intruder. I had not noticed I had stepped into her territory." He paused for a few moments.

"Go on." I urged him.

"I immediately got attacked. Obviously, it was fine. Your mother did not land a strike. However, after I explained who I was, we got to talking. She told me about her pack, and her two children; your brother and sister." He said with a smile.

"We saw each other for a few months after that. Sadly, once she found out she was pregnant with you, Hera was getting extremely angry with me. I was also ignoring my duty as king of the gods. So, I reluctantly returned to Olympus. I was able to keep you and your mother safe and in secret. However, as we know, my brother, your uncle, Hades, found out, and attempted to kill you."

"And now, I'm fighting for my life, left my pack, and traveled across the country just to almost die fighting Hades," I said a chill in my voice.

"I am very sorry for that, Jensen. You will no longer need to worry about Hades."

"Good."

"However, from what Apollo tells me, your troubles are not over?" Zeus continued.

"How so?" I said, more interested now than I was a few moments ago.

"Sadly, I cannot elaborate. Revealing too much of the future can cause people to attempt to change it. That only leads to death."

I was silent for a few moments, processing.

"Can you at least tell me when this is going to happen?" I asked.

"Soon. Very, very soon." He said intensely.

"One more thing," I said.

"Yes?"

"I need you to apologize to Penny for killing Ajax. Also, stop killing werewolves for no reason."

Zeus stood there for a few moments before responding.

"As you wish."

Before we could continue the conversation, however, Penny yelled my name from across the room.

"Jensen! We need to go!" Hermes was standing next to her, a look of worry on his face.

I ran over to my friends, Zeus right behind me.

"What's going on?" I asked.

Hermes was the one that answered.

"Your camp is in danger." He said flatly.

I spun on Zeus.

"Hades? I thought you said he wouldn't be a problem." Instinctively, I extended my claws.

"No, Jensen!" Hermes warned, grabbing my shoulder. "Do not blame our father. It is not Hades causing problems."

"Who then?" I spun on Hermes, who took his hand away quickly.

"You won't believe me. You must see for yourself, brother."

Hermes snapped his fingers and a portal opened behind his right shoulder. "Hurry."

My friends and I rushed through the portal. When we arrived at school, it all looked normal. We ran passed the SUV Leo had rented to take us to D.C. and through the gates. As we ascended the steps, the doors flung open.

"Jensen!" Marchessa said in surprise.

"What's going on?" I asked, slightly out of breath.

"Nothing. Weren't you on Olympus?" Her glowing red eyes scanned our group.

"We were," Megan answered. "Hermes sent us back. He said there was a problem."

Marchessa looked around the area, her eyes acting like spotlights.

"I see and sense nothing. Calm down, come inside."

As if on queue, I heard a distinctive howl in the distance.

My claws extended.

"Get inside. Get the school ready."

"What's going on?" Penny asked, spinning her ring on her finger.

"Wolves," I mumbled. "Very big wolves. Get inside. Now." It was not a request.

"I'm staying with you," Penny said as the others filed past us.

I looked around the campus and saw no other students. Checking my watch, I noticed it was about lunchtime. I spun on Marchessa.

"Tell no one to leave the school. Create a phalanx at the doors. Be prepared."

Marchessa nodded and ran after my friends.

Penny was still standing next to me.

"If you're going to stay, then I need you to do something," I told her. "Have the river flow towards the gates. We're going to need it."

She nodded and ran off to the river.

I sprinted toward the gate, fully shifting as I went. The gates were still hanging wide open. Again, I heard a howl, about a mile closer. They were closing in quickly, moving even faster than I could. I felt the same force as before, pulling me in the direction of the howl. Internally, my werewolf side was fighting with my human side. I had to concentrate to not shift.

A few moments later, Penny was at my side. I heard running water a few feet behind me.

"River is redirected. What's happening?" She sounded worried.

"Werewolves. A lot of them, and they're fast."

"How fast?"

"Faster than me."

Penny frowned.

"How is that possible." It wasn't a question.

"I can only think of one way. Either it's a pack of nothing but alphas, which shouldn't be possible, or it's something much, much worse."

"What?"

I didn't have time to explain.

Before I could say anything, the woods to our right exploded. Trees flew in every direction. Leaves rained down on top of us.

In front of us stood at least two dozen werewolves. However, they weren't like me. These wolves stood fifteen feet tall, taller than any hellhound I have seen. They were pure black, except for their eyes. The wolf in the front, who was bigger than the rest by at least ten feet, had the same glowing eyes as an alpha.

"Lycaon?" I asked, even though I was sure of the answer.

The wolf started to transform. It shrank to average human height.

The man that now stood in front of me had long black hair past his shoulders. When he smiled, I noticed his teeth were a sickly yellow color and covered with blood. His eyes were still glowing bright red.

"Yes, little beta."

I growled.

"What are you doing here? No one has seen teeth or tail of you in a century."

"I came for you, Jensen." Lycaon laughed. "You are the youngest of my descendants, and the most powerful." The alpha turned his eyes to Penny. "I see you have made some friends."

Instinctively, I moved in front of Penny.

"You leave her alone."

Lycaon started pacing slowly, his hands behind his back.

"Now, Jensen, I have no intention of hurting anyone. That is unless you refuse my offer.

If that's the case, then I will be forced to kill you and your entire school."

"Over my dead body." Anger surged through my body, it was becoming harder to control my werewolf side. Every ounce of my concentration was focused on being human.

"Oh, rest assured, that can be arranged. Although I would hate for that to happen." Lycaon continued to pace.

"What offer are you talking about?" I asked.

"Well, I would like for you to join my pack, Jensen."

I actually laughed. Finally, what I've been feeling recently had made sense. Everywhere I went, the Immortals were following me, trying to pull me toward them. Tempting me to join their pack.

"How could you think I would do that? I know of the Immortals. You're all just savage killing machines. I'll never be one of you."

Lycaon did not look deterred.

"Think about it, beta, immortality. More power than you could ever think of. An endless source of wolves. I would make you my delta. You would live beyond normal life and gain riches past your wildest dreams. How can you pass this up?" He stopped in front of me, smiling.

"Yes, and for me to have all of this, I would have to kill innocent people."

"Oh, please. First off, no one is innocent. Secondly, we only kill those who pose a threat. Well, other than the occasional meal. However, those only happen once a week now. Plus, if we didn't kill, the human population would push the limits of the planet. We're doing a good deed for the world."

However, maybe he had a point. If I joined him, my friends would be safe. I would have everything a person could want. I pondered this for a few moments. Maybe it was because he was the first Immortal, and we were directly connected, but I wanted to join him. I wanted him to turn me immortal. Then the thought of killing innocent people came crashing to the forefront of my mind.

"Too much killing for me. No dice." I arched my back, ready for a fight. "We going to do this or not, Lycaon?"

Lycaon started to pace again, his wolves in the background started getting agitated.

"Jensen, you do realize, if you fight, you and your friend will die, don't you."

"You wish," Penny said from behind me.

"Lycaon, I promise, if you hurt her, or anyone else in this school, it will be the last thing you will ever do." I threatened.

Lycaon barked out a laugh.

"We are immortal, Jensen. You cannot kill us. I will use your friend's bones to pick my

teeth." He said with a sneer.

That was it. I couldn't listen to these psychopathic delusions anymore. I pounced.

16

Chapter Sixteen: The Immortals

This was probably the dumbest thing I could have ever done.

Once I leaped towards Lycaon, he shifted into his wolf form in a blink of an eye. With one motion he swatted me to the side. I flew to the left and crashed through a series of trees. They crashed down on top of me and I felt my ribs crack. However, I didn't have time to register the pain.

I pushed the trees off of me and ran back through the path my body made. Just in time, I leaped and slammed into Lycaon with all my strength. A few moments before, the alpha wolf was bounding down on Penny, who had summoned her trident and was backing into the wall.

Lycaon was lifted off of his feet and soared through the air. Bad move Jensen.

Once their alpha hit the ground, the other wolves attacked. Thankfully, they were just betas. I lifted a nearby tree and swung it like a baseball bat.

The six wolves in the lead were knocked sideways and landed next to Lycaon. I swung the tree in the opposite direction and took out another three. With the little breathing room I had, I looked back at Penny.

"River. Water. Now!" I yelled.

Penny lifted her trident in the air and I heard a rumbling coming from behind the wall. A few moments later, a wall of water came crashing down. The remaining wolves washed away, yelping in pain. The water was churning, causing them not to be able to move. Penny forced the water away a few hundred yards and froze the werewolves into a block of ice.

"You okay?" I asked, looking at the agony on her face.

"I will be later. Still getting used to these powers." She said, out of breath. "Don't worry about me, you've got bigger problems."

She was right. Across the clearing in front of the gates, Lycaon and his betas were getting up and they did not look happy.

Lycaon was the first one on his feet. He glared at me and snarled. Before I could react, he charged me. Now, the first werewolf was not as fast as the giant Damysus, but he was faster than me.

Lycaon cleared the distance between us in two seconds flat. Once in front of me, he slammed his paw into my chest and pinned me to the ground, his claws in my shoulders. Blood started pouring from the wounds. Steam started rising from Lycaon's claws. I yelled in pain.

"Jensen!" Penny screamed. "Ypostírixi! Support, now!" She yelled behind her.

"No!" I roared, drowning out Penny's plea for help.

With all of my strength, I dug my claws into Lycaon's leg and lifted. To my surprise, the wolf was lifted off the ground. As he yelped in pain, even though it was pushing my strength to its limit, I threw him.

He slammed into his betas as they were charging in to help. Penny dropped to her knees, resting the butt of her trident on the ground. I ran to her side.

"Everything okay?"

"Fine. Just catching my breath." She got to her feet, looking perfectly fine. No time to worry about her, even though I was worried.

"What other tricks can that trident do?" I asked, wincing as I turned. My shoulder wounds were not healing as quickly as they should have been.

"Let's find out." She said and raised the weapon above her head.

As the wolves were running toward us, she slammed the prongs of the trident into the ground. There was a slight pause, then the earth started to shake. Bricks feel out of the wall. One of the gates shook off its hinges and fell to the ground. Behind us, the school was shaking as well. Shingles fell from the roof.

Under my feet, the ground started to crack. I looked at Penny, who was now pale white. Sweat was dripping down her face. Her eyes were bloodshot from the effort.

The longer she had her trident in the ground, the more intense the earthquake became. However, it was working. The wolves were now extremely off-balance, but Lycaon himself had his eyes on Penny. I ran to meet him as he began to move toward her.

He was too quick. I attempted to bring my claws along his flank, but he moved, and I missed. Once he was past me, Penny was wide open.

I watched as if in slow motion. The other wolves gathered around me in a circle. Lycaon was on top of Penny now. He brought his trash can lid sized paw down on her chest. I watched as his claws sank through her shoulders and chest. The claws drilled themselves into the ground. Penny screamed in pain, but it was drowned by the blood pumping through my veins.

I had no idea what I was doing. For the second time that day, I was overcome with pure rage. Vaguely, I noticed clouds gathering over me and turning a deep grey, like a forming storm. The wind picked up around me, as it did right before I fought Heracles. Thunder shook the sky above my head. Before I knew what was happening, I yelled in anger.

Lightning came from the sky, but not just one bolt. Six bolts of lightning came and struck the enemies around me. I heard the Immortals yelp in pain. Around me, I saw a fire, as if the wolves were dissolving. I didn't think that was possible, but I didn't question my good luck.

Next, I reached into my pocket and pull out my flashlight. I threw it with all my might at Lycaon. While it was halfway through its journey, I channeled a small lightning bolt through it and transformed it into a spear.

Just as Lycaon was turning around to address the noises, the spear struck him in the chest. He howled in pain. Silver blood, ichor, poured from the wound.

The alpha regained his balance after being pushed backward by my attack. Using his paw, he swatted the spear from his chest. It skidded across the ground. The rain started to fall from the clouds I had summoned. In seconds, I was soaked.

I looked at Penny, and she was dripping wet. She wasn't moving, definitely knocked out. Even more, anger surged through me.

Running as fast as I could, I charged Lycaon. He was expecting me, the wound in his chest already healed.

The alpha snapped his jaws at me, but I was able to dodge underneath him. I slashed my claws against his stomach. Again, I saw more ichor. However, once I had pulled my hand away, the wound closed, leaving no trace of my blow. Spinning around behind him, I jumped over his back. This time, he was too quick for me.

As I fell through the air, about to land on the ground, Lycaon snatched me in his jaws.

Pain filled my body, however, my anger was numbing it. I jabbed my claws into Lycaons eyes. Immediately, he dropped me.

As ichor flowed from his eye sockets, and the wounds attempted to close, Lycaon stumbled backward into the wall. I ran over and picked Penny and her trident up. She was cold, covered in blood and growing even paler.

Quickly, while Lycaon recovered, I jumped over the wall and ran to the front doors of the

school.

"Open up! It's me! Penny's hurt!" I yelled.

There were a few clicks and what sounded like wood moving. A few seconds later,

the doors flew open. In front of me stood a fully formed phalanx that was three demigods thick. Every student in the school was standing there, waiting to defend their home.

A small hole opened in the phalanx and Megan and Rachael came running up to me. Together they took Penny from my arms.

"Fix her," I told Megan, and she nodded.

Rachael's gaze, however, was focused behind me. I turned around and saw Lycaon stumbling around, waiting for his eyes to heal. Every now and then he would let out a howl. Suddenly, an idea popped into my head.

"Rachael. Silver. I need silver." I told her.

From behind her, Rob was the one that answered.

"In the forges. There's a silver poker that we use to shape some weapons.

It's really sharp."

I nodded and left Penny with my friends.

"Close the doors. Do not open them until I say so."

I ran toward the forges and heard the doors close and lock behind me. As I ran, I noticed Lycaon had recovered. He barrelled down on me with blinding speed. His eyes seemed to glow more intensely. He let out another howl, and I stopped in my tracks, wanting to run towards the alpha.

I was ten feet from the doors to the forges. Suddenly, a sharp pain shot through my leg, starting in my calf. When I turned, I saw Lycaon had sunk his teeth into me. I fell to the ground.

The wounds on my chest still hadn't healed fully. Now, my leg was gushing blood. Lycaon released his jaws and stood over me.

I looked behind me, through the doors of the forges. Sitting in a corner was a large silver poker. Judging by the look on his face, Lycaon hadn't noticed it.

Before my eyes, he changed back to human.

"Jensen, you should have accepted my offer. You might have dispatched some of my wolves, but they will be back. The ice cannot hold them forever."

"You forget, I fried six of them. What makes you think I can't do the same to you?" I said, adding a growl to my voice.

Lycaon laughed.

"I'm much harder to kill than my betas. Simple lightning won't do."

I decided to challenge his theory and stabbed my claws into Lycaons chest and channeled electricity through them. The alpha flew backward but was still on his feet, his chest smoking. As quick as I could, I got to my feet.

Turning around and using the wind, I summoned the silver poker to my hand. When I turned back around, for the first time, Lycaon actually looked scared.

"Now, Jensen, let's talk about this. Even if you stab me with that, it will not kill me forever. I will return." He held his hands up in a pleading gesture.

I stumbled towards him, swing the poker like a sword. It was incredibly unbalanced, but I managed to make it look intimidating. As I limped closer to Lycaon, he backed up.

The only thing that could hurt him was in my hand. Silver, if you didn't know, has always been a weakness to werewolves in stories. That's not true for modern werewolves, like me, but for the Immortals, such as Lycaon, it was very much true.

Every step I took, my ancestor looked more and more terrified. Sweat started pouring down his face. The rain was still falling from the sky, but I could tell this was different. He seemed on the verge of tears.

"You hurt someone I care about very much," I said, swinging the poker again. "You threatened my new home. You tried to trick me into becoming a killer." Lycaon stumbled backward and landed on his back, his hands still in front of him, trying to protect himself.

"Please. Don't kill me. I hate Tartarus!"

"You try to recruit me into being an immortal killing machine!" I was yelling now, I vaguely heard the doors to the school open, but I ignored it.

I was now limping over to Lycaon who was scurrying backward on his hands.

"I'm sorry. If you let me live, I promise, I will not return!" He was begging now. I could hear his heartbeat, and instantly knew he was lying.

I stood over him, the poker hovering over his heart.

"Tell me, what were you planning Lycaon?"

I sliced the poker across his chest, leaving a smoking, bleeding mark. Lycaon yelped in pain.

"Nothing!" Again, he was lying.

"I know you're lying, alpha! Tell. Me. The truth." With every word, I slashed the poker across his skin, leaving more smoky cuts.

Deep inside of me, I knew Lycaon was planning something. I didn't know how I knew this, I just did. It didn't make sense that he would just show up here. It didn't make sense that he would come to look for me. I could believe he knew about me, being the first werewolf, he was connected to all of us, but why show up here? Now?

Sadly, I had gotten too cocky. Lycaon grabbed the poker in his hand, stood up, and sank his claws into my stomach. He moved his head right next to my ear. I could feel his silver ichor flow over me.

"You're lucky you've injured me, beta, or you would be dead. All you need

178

to know about my plans is that the world will crumble. Your father will die."

He pulled his claws away and I fell to the ground, holding my stomach. Judging by my experience with the other wounds Lycaon had given me, it seemed that if I'm injured by an alpha, it takes longer to heal. Out of the corner of my eye, I saw Lycaon shift back into his wolf form and run away, disappearing in the forest. Past the gates, I noticed the wolves that were encased in ice start to dissolve into shadows and disappear.

In the distance, I heard people yelling my name, but my vision was getting blurry. Blood continued to flow from the wounds all over my body. My shoulders were more or less healed, but the injury happened almost an hour ago at this point. If it took that long for everything else to heal, I was in big trouble.

Someone grabbed me by my shoulders and set my head on their lap. I could make out a black hair girl above me and a red-headed girl going through a bag. Before I could say or do anything, I blacked out.

When I woke up a few hours later, well, I thought it was a few hours, there was a very big commotion going on. I heard Megan yelling at someone and a deep booming voice yelling back. Whenever the man yelled, the walls would shake. Also, I heard another, less imposing voice. Both of these men sounded familiar.

"Let me talk to him." Said the first man.

"My lord, he needs rest," Megan said.

"Daughter, please, this is a grave matter. I know you feel it too." The second man told Megan. That was obviously Apollo.

There was silence for a few moments before Megan answered.

"Fine. Please, Lord Zeus, be quick. He was seriously injured."

I heard footsteps coming down the hall. When I opened my eyes, I noticed I was laying in the infirmary. My shirt was off and my midsection was wrapped in bandages. Looking to my left, I saw Penny in the bed next to me. Before I could even try to get out of bed to check on her, the doors to the infirmary opened.

When I looked over, my father was walking to my bedside, closely followed by Apollo, and surprisingly, Hermes.

"Jensen! Are you okay?" Zeus asked, reaching my bed.

I propped myself up on my pillows.

"I've been better." I looked at Hermes. "Thank you for the warning."

The messenger god nodded.

Apollo placed his hand over my stomach.

"Your wounds seemed to have healed. Considering you have been unconscious for six hours, I'm not surprised. My daughter made us wait before seeing you."

I looked over at Penny, who was still there, motionless in her bed.

"Lord Apollo," I said, addressing the sun god. "Can you heal her?"

Apollo walked over to Penny's bed. He looked her up and down, then snapped his fingers. Penny moaned a little in her sleep, then exhaled.

"She'll be fine. Werewolf wounds are difficult to heal, however, for me, it is no trouble." Apollo explained, walking back to my bedside.

"Thank you, Apollo," I said, sitting up a little straighter.

"Now, son," Zeus said. "I need to know what happened with Lycaon. All of it." He had a very serious look on his face.

I told my father everything that happened. How Lycaon just showed up out of nowhere, attempted to recruit me, and finally, our fight. I left out being tempted to join him.

"After we were done," I was saying, "He tried to take the poker from me. He said 'The world will crumble. Your father will die.' Then he ran away."

Zeus did not look happy. Rage and worry poured over his face. He turned to Hermes.

"My son, go to Olympus. Inform Athena that the second war is soon going to begin. Call a council. Apollo and I will be along in a few minutes."

Hermes gave Zeus a slight bow.

"Yes, my lord." He said, and then he dissolved into white mist.

"Jensen, I'm sorry to say that your work is not done," Apollo said. "We may need your assistance again very soon."

"I figured as much." I joked. "Let me know when and where," I told my father.

Zeus nodded.

"Oh, Penelope." Zeus addressed Penny. "I'm very sorry about my previous actions that involved you."

Penny just sat there for a few seconds. She couldn't seem to speak, so she settled for nodding.

"One more thing before we go, Jensen. We have some people who would like to see you." My father said.

Zeus stepped back to reveal the door. When it opened, my mother was standing there. She ran inside, pushed the king of the gods out of the way and wrapped me in a hug.

"Jensen! I was so worried about you. Are you okay? Lycaon? How is that even possible?" She said all of this within a second.

"I'm fine, mom. I promise."

Over her shoulder, I saw two other people standing there. Zak and Stephanie made their way through the room. When they passed Zeus and Apollo, they looked at them as if terrified.

"They're okay," I told them. "Promise."

My mother let me go to make way for my siblings. Stephanie gave me a hug and Zak patted my arm.

"Are you coming home?" Zak asked me.

I was silent for a few moments. To be honest, I hadn't thought of that. My plan was to stay here, train a little more, protect my friends. Apollo had just told me they are probably going to need me. From what it sounds like, Lycaon was going to attack Olympus. I couldn't just stand by and do nothing.

"You don't need to." My mother said softly. "You can stay here if you want."

Again, I was silent. My head was foggy while I was thinking. The only thing that brought me back to reality was Penny. She groaned and moved around in her bed. Her eyes opened.

"Megan!" I yelled, swinging my legs out of bed, pushing Zak and my mother aside.

Megan came running into the infirmary, medical bag in hand.

"Are you okay? What hurts?" She asked Penny when she reached her bed.

"I'm fine. Just a little groggy." Penny pushed herself up on to her pillows. She scanned the room at the weird scene in front of her.

"Lord Apollo. Lord Zeus." She said respectfully. She made eye contact with my mother. "Who's this?" She asked, raising an eyebrow.

"Penny, this is my mother and my brother and sister." I introduced them. "Guys, this is Penelope Conway. Daughter of Poseidon."

My mother shook Penny's hand.

"Nice to meet you, dear." She said, looking at Penny then at me. A slight smile danced across her face.

"This is too weird," Stephanie said. "We're going to wait outside." She grabbed Zak by the shoulder and steered him out of the room.

"Gods," Zak muttered, shaking his head.

"Anyway." Zeus began. "Apollo and I must return to Olympus. Lydia, it was nice to see you again."

"Very nice, Lord Zeus." My mother said, outstretching her hand.

Zeus took it and shook.

"Jensen, my son, I will send word with Hermes if you are needed. Even if you wish to return home."

I nodded and shook my father's hand.

"Until we meet again." Zeus waved his hand and dissolved into the same white mist as Hermes had.

Apollo was the only god remaining. He walked up to Megan and gave her a hug.

"Don't forget the unicorn horn." I heard him whisper in her ear.

After he broke away from Megan, he said his goodbyes. Then, he too, dissolved into mist.

I looked at Penny and Megan for a few moments. A realization was sinking in that they needed me here.

"Mother, I'll come back for the summer, but I'm going to stay here until then. They need me." I said without even thinking.

"I understand, little beta." She gripped my hand. "As long as you're happy and safe."

I laughed.

"Yeah, mom, I'm going to be safe fighting Lycaon and a thousand other monsters."

My mother smiled.

"You'll be fine." She said, letting go of my hand. "Just visit when summer comes around."

"I will. I promise."

My mother gave me another hug.

"I'll wait for you outside. Come to see us off, will you?"

I nodded.

My mother walked out of the infirmary and closed the door behind her. I turned to Megan.

"Can I have a little time with Penny, please?" I asked her.

She looked around nervously.

"Sure thing, Jensen." She too left the room.

Penny and I sat alone in silence for a few moments.

"I thought you were going to die, Penny," I mumbled.

I wasn't making eye contact with her. Honestly, I didn't want her to look me in the eyes. In my mind, I thought I would start crying.

Penny swung her legs off her bed and placed her hand on mine.

"You saved me." She whispered. "It was my decision to stay with you. You got me out of there alive."

"It was my fault you were hurt in the first place. I was too slow." I admitted.

"No, Jensen. None of that was your fault." She put her other hand under my chin and lifted my face up to meet hers. "You are the most amazing demigod I have ever seen. Not only have you gone toe-to-toe with gods, but you also faced the oldest and most powerful werewolf in history. Both times you walked way in victory. No one else could have done that."

I heard her heartbeat increase. Excitement bubbling up inside her.

"I don't know what I would have done if you would have died," I told her. "Ever since I came to school, you and I have gotten really close. Now, I couldn't imagine life without you."

Penny's face grew bright red.

"What about Rachael?" She asked nervously.

"She's a really good friend. A great friend actually, but I click with you more. I guess." Now I was getting nervous.

"You're an idiot." She smiled and leaned in.

The next second, she was kissing me.

17

Chapter Seventeen: Until next time

Penny and I were interrupted by a knock on the door. We broke apart. Penny's face was still red, but she was smiling.

"Come in!" I called.

Rachael opened the door, two cards in her hand. She walked over and handed them to us.

"Get well cards." She said sheepishly.

Her eyes were fixed on my hand. I then realized that Penny's hand was still on mine. We quickly separated.

"Thanks, Rachael, I appreciate that," Penny said, giving Rachael a hug.

"How are you guys feeling?" Rachael asked.

"I'm fine. Penny still has to rest. Apollo healed her, but he said she should stay in bed." I explained.

"I think Apollo was right," Penny said, wincing as she tried to get up. "Bed sounds good."

"I'm going to go see my family off." I got up and pulled on a fresh shirt, which I guess Megan had grabbed from my room. "We'll talk later?" I asked Penny.

"Most definitely." She answered.

As I left, and Rachael's back was turned, I mouthed to Penny to talk to Rachael. Hopefully, she got the message.

When I walked through the doors, Megan was standing off to the left.

"You can go in," I told her, and she walked inside.

At the end of the hall, by the doorway to the stairs, my family stood there talking to Leo and Marchessa. When I walked up, Leo locked eyes with me and smiled.

"Jensen! Your family is a delight."

"They're okay." Marchessa agreed.

"That's a compliment coming from her," I whispered to my brother.

He laughed.

We all walked onto the stairs. I jumped over the banister and landed on the ground. Everyone else decided to play it safe and walk down the steps.

"When did you get so adventurous?" Stephanie asked me when they made it to the bottom.

"Don't know," I answered.

I walked my family to the gates outside. The sun was now hanging low in the sky, and the clouds I had summoned had evaporated. Rob and a few of his brothers were fixing the gate that had collapsed. He waved from the top of the wall as he secured the highest hinge.

"I'll see you in a few weeks," I told my mother, hugging her.

"I better." She responded. "Be safe."

My mother shook hands with Leo and Marchessa, as did my brother and sister. I hugged my siblings, and without any other words, they all shifted and ran toward the woods. As they disappeared into the darkness, I was thinking about how much I was going to miss them over the next few weeks.

I was snapped back to earth by a tap on my shoulder. It was Rachael.

"Penny told me what happened." She said, flatly.

"Oh." I rubbed the nape of my neck awkwardly. "I'm sorry."

"Don't be." I noticed that she wasn't nervous anymore. Her heartbeat was steady. "I just had a crush. I'm over it now."

How can you get over a crush that quickly? I thought.

There was silence again for about a minute while we stood there. I was starting to get used to awkward silences.

"She really likes you, you know?" Rachael mentioned suddenly.

"I thought so. I like her too." I finally admitted.

It felt good to get that out. I haven't even admitted that to myself. Over the last few weeks, Penny and I had really gotten close. We spent a lot of time together. We talked constantly. The feelings just sort of popped up.

"Don't let the Aphrodite kids find out you two are together. They'll lose their minds. They've been talking about you two getting together for weeks." Rachael informed me, jokingly. Thankfully, she was smiling.

"Well, I don't know if we'll get together, but you never know," I told her.

She rolled her eyes and lightly punched me in the arm.

"You're stupid." She said and started to walk away. "See you at dinner."

Rob dropped down from his post on top of the gate and walked over to me. He pointed to the forges, where his bike was sitting.

"Hermes dropped it off. I know you were worried about it." He said sarcastically.

"Oh, so worried man. First thing on my mind when I woke up, actually."

Rob laughed and walked back over to his siblings, who were still working on the gate.

As I stood there alone, I looked up into the sky. Apollo said that they would need me. Zeus deduced that Lycaon was planning an attack on Olympus. I was supposed to be a part of that. Lycaon wanted me to become immortal. Was I supposed to fend off the Immortals on my own? I had no idea if I could do that, but I might have to try.

Thinking about it again, I was still slightly tempted. However, I trusted myself to protect my friends. I hoped my trust in myself wasn't misplaced.

Hopefully, the next school year was easier.

Made in the USA
Middletown, DE
17 February 2020

84785718R00116